# POSING AS
# Ashley

Posing as Ashley
Text © 2008 Kimberly Joy Peters

Published by Lobster Press™
1620 Sherbrooke Street West, Suites C & D
Montréal, Québec  H3H 1C9
Tel. (514) 904-1100 • Fax (514) 904-1101 • www.lobsterpress.com

Publisher: Alison Fripp
Editor: Meghan Nòlan
Editorial Assistants: Emma Stephen & Brynn Smith-Raska
Proofreader: Mahak Jain
Graphic Design & Production: Tammy Desnoyers

We acknowledge the financial support of the Government of Canada through the Book Publishing Industry Development Program (BPIDP) for our publishing activities.

The Canada Council | Le Conseil des Arts
for the Arts | du Canada

We acknowledge the support of the Canada Council for the Arts for our publishing program.

Library and Archives Canada Cataloguing in Publication

Peters, Kimberly Joy, 1969-
    Posing as Ashley / Kimberly Joy Peters.

ISBN 978-1-897073-87-2

    I. Title.

PS8631.E823P68 2008        jC813'.6        C2008-901097-3

Printed and bound in Canada.

Text is printed on Rolland Enviro 100 Book, 100% recycled post-consumer fibre.

*For Randy, who taught me so much about perseverance,
and Honey, who was beautiful inside and out.*

– Kimberly Joy Peters

# POSING AS Ashley

written by
## Kimberly Joy Peters

Lobster Press ™

# CHAPTER 1

I was the girl you wanted to hate. People joked about it, but I know it was true. They wanted to hate me because I was the girl they thought they couldn't be: the *smart* one, the *pretty* one, the *nice* one, the one with the *great boyfriend*.

Before I started modeling, that's what they saw, because that's all I showed them. The real stuff – the stuff inside – I kept hidden. I hid it because the imperfections that might have made me seem more human were the things that sometimes made me hate myself.

* * *

Though he caught the occasional glimpse of it, even my boyfriend, Brandon, didn't really know how much the deeper things, like my fear of never being good enough, shaped the outside Ashley that I portrayed to the rest of the world.

Brandon and I went out for almost two years. He has these amazing brown eyes and dark hair, but the thing I always liked best about him, right from the beginning, was that he was smart and that he wasn't intimidated by the fact that I always try to do my best at everything, too. All my life, kids have made snide comments about my academic abilities – I've been called names like "Brown Noser" and "Teacher's Pet" – which I never worried about, because I knew that most of it came out of jealousy. The part of me that's always doing my best is worth more than other people's jealousy, and Brandon got that, right from the start.

Even though he always said he loved the way I look – especially my long, thick dark hair – he was equally proud of the fact that I didn't try to coast by on my looks, pretending to be dumb, like a lot of other girls do.

Everyone thought we were the perfect couple. *I* thought we were the perfect couple. And I know that at one point, *he* believed it too. But at the beginning of the summer, Brandon changed his mind.

School had just ended for the year, and I'd thought we were going to hang out together – just the two of us – because he was leaving the next day to work at a canoe camp for the summer months. We'd planned to go to a movie, and I expected that it would be followed by a make-out session in his mom's car and a tearful goodbye with promises to write every day.

"Let's not go to the movie," he said when he picked me up. "Let's go sit out on the hill and talk."

I'd never seen him so serious, so I ran through possible "talking topics" in my mind, hoping maybe my suspicions were wrong. My mom had recently had surgery for breast cancer and I was scared for her, but Brandon and I talked about that all the time – he didn't need to make it a special issue.

I also wondered if it had anything to do with him going away – because he wouldn't have a cell phone or email access at camp – but we'd already been over that too. Neither one of us is insecure or jealous, and he'd actually said he was looking forward to getting real letters with lipstick kisses – letters that smelled like me.

Though it didn't make sense, I tried to prepare myself for what I suspected might be coming next. We'd always had a great connection and had been able to tell each other anything, but we'd never started any conversations with "Let's talk." *Everyone* knows what that means.

"Okay," I said, reaching for his hand in the car. I thought I felt him jump just a bit when I touched him. "What's wrong?"

He glanced at me quickly, then down at our hands, before returning his gaze to the road and his hand to the wheel. "Your hands are all scratched," he said.

I didn't believe that that was the problem, but I explained: "We got a new litter of kittens at the animal shelter today, and they're at the perfect age for play-fighting."

"How many are there?" He seemed to relax slightly. I'd been volunteering at the shelter for five months and he liked hearing all about the animals.

"Six. Their mother is a little black cat named Raven, so I just slid one letter down in the alphabet and gave them all *s* names: Samson, Smokey, Sox, Sophie, Stella, and Sacha. Most of them are gray tabbies, but Samson and Sacha are black, like their mother."

Then I got quiet, wondering what Brandon really wanted to discuss, but I'm sure he just thought my mind was still back at the shelter.

"You'll find homes for them, Ash, even the all-black cats." He reached over and gave my hand a squeeze. As much as I always try to give off the impression of confidence in everything I do, I loved that he knew what I was worried about and that he wanted to comfort me. Black cats are the hardest ones to find homes for, even though some people consider them *good* luck and Julius Caesar is rumored to have kept one for that reason. I'd cried on Brandon's shoulder many times about the ones we couldn't place.

I'd always known I wanted to be a vet, and I hoped that someday when I was, I'd be able to offer low-cost clinics to spay and neuter people's pets. It was Brandon who'd suggested that to me – the idea of keeping the price down – when I'd started to get discouraged by the overflow of animals at the shelter. He often inspired me in that way, and I knew it was part of what I would miss the most while he was gone this summer.

We sat in silence during the rest of the drive to the school and then walked together up a hill beside the field where I always sit to watch his football games.

"So?" I began.

"So, what?" he said, suddenly playing dumb. But I knew he had something on his mind.

"So what do we need to talk about?" I prodded, anxious to get things moving, regardless of which direction they were about to take.

"You. Us ..." his voice trailed off, and I swear I felt my heart breaking into a million pieces at that very moment. He went on to tell me all the things every girl wants to hear: how "amazing" I am; how I'm an "incredible combination of beauty, brains, and personality"; how "proud" he was to be my boyfriend; and how "great" the last couple of years had been.

When he'd finished the inventory of my good qualities, he started staring off into space, really intently. He wasn't looking at me, but at the goalposts out in the football field. It was as if he was being paid to watch them, should they become alive and try to make a break for it and escape out into the woods. I couldn't help but think that maybe he was wishing *he* could make a break for it and escape into the woods – because he knew what he was about to tell me, and he knew me well enough to know how I would react.

While he talked, I had such a sharp, excruciating pain deep down into my gut, that I thought for a second that there was something physically wrong with me. But then I realized that I wasn't breathing and that every part of my body was clenched tight.

"So are you actually going to come out and say it?" I finally asked in a small, measured voice that I almost didn't recognize as my own.

"Ashley – "

"You have to say it. You owe me that," I insisted, my voice hardly shaking, but my insides crawling now as if I was full of maggots. "You have to at least say it out loud."

"Ashley, you know I love you ..." he said. I could feel the biggest "but" of my life hesitating right there, on the edge of his lips, afraid to come out and meet me head-on.

"But I don't think we should be a couple anymore ... right now," he finished.

"So are you *dumping* me?" I asked without looking at him.

"No – I'm not dumping you. I still want to date you – sometimes – but I'm just saying that with me going away for the summer, we shouldn't be, you know, boyfriend/girlfriend anymore. We should both be free to see other people."

I felt as if I'd been tossed out of a moving car.

# CHAPTER 2

While Brandon talked, I tried to keep breathing.

When he paused, I demanded specifics. "What do you mean by 'see other people'?" I was pressing him for answers, and I knew it was possibly going to make him mad, but at the very least, I deserved some explanation. I wasn't going to let him off easily.

"You know – just, like, go out with people of the opposite sex, like to a movie or something."

"We already do that," I said, still pressing. Each of us had friends of the opposite sex, and neither of us had any problem with that. We just didn't kiss them or hold their hands or do anything else considered romantic. "So what I want to know is, *who* do you want to be going to the movies with?"

"What do you mean, 'who?'" He was still staring at the goalposts.

My voice got very quiet, which I didn't intend. I wanted to be strong, but I said it again. "Look me in the eye and tell me *who* it is that you want to be able to go out with."

"Nobody. Honest, Ashley." He was looking at me, finally, and I could see he was upset too. That counted for something. "It's just that with me going away and everything, I wouldn't want to feel like I was, you know, cheating on you, if I *did* end up taking someone out."

I was furious, but I let him continue.

"Plus," he said, "my mom thinks we should take a break for a bit."

"Your *mom*? This is about your *mom*? Since when does she have any say in *our* relationship?"

"Since she read some of our emails."

I didn't have to ask which ones. We'd been together long enough that there were lots of emails I didn't want shared with anyone. His mother would be the worst possible audience.

"How did she get into your email?" Although it wasn't the most important question at the moment, it was one that I could focus on.

He hesitated. "I ... I just left the account open and when she went to borrow my computer to print something, she saw them."

"But you're always so careful to shut everything down – "

"Look – I don't know all the details," he said, cutting me off. "I just think it would be good for us to take a break – for the summer, at least."

"You did tell her we're not having sex, didn't you?" I asked, feeling embarrassed and violated at the thought of someone reading our private correspondence.

"What? I'm not going to tell her that! And, anyway, she never said anything about sex. Just that we're too young to be getting so serious. And maybe she's right," he added, as if he'd just thought of it.

Now I was the one staring at the goalposts. "She thinks we're having sex, and that's what she means when she says we're 'too serious.' You have to tell her we're not sleeping together."

"It's just for the summer, Ash. I still care about you and we can still write and we'll probably end up stronger when I get home – I just need to take a bit of a break ... so my mom will back off."

"I won't do 'a break,'" I said, even though I knew equally well that I didn't want him to change his mind and stay with me just because I wouldn't agree to his terms. Not being with him would be horrible, but staying together if *he* didn't want to be with *me* would be worse.

"What do you mean you 'won't do a break?'" He'd finally started to cry, but I was determined not to. I had to show him I would be okay without him. I wasn't going to let him see how much he was hurting me. And I *certainly* wasn't going to let him change all the rules and go against everything that made sense to me by slinking off quietly for the summer just so it would make things easier for him and his snooping mother!

"I mean that if you really love me," I said, "like you say you do, then we both know you're making a big mistake. But at least have the decency to break up with me *now* and not drag it out by saying you want to see other people over the summer so you can dump me when you get back in August. You can't have it both ways – 'dating' me when it's convenient for you, but not being my boyfriend."

"Look," he said, trying to reason with me, "I know my timing sucks, with your mom being sick and everything – "

"Don't you *dare* bring her into this!" I spat. When he reached out to touch my arm, I quickly shoved it away.

He looked as if he was going to be sick, but he continued. "I just mean that I know you're already under a lot of stress and I don't want to add to it. But it makes sense to take a break now – when I'm going to be away anyhow, and then you can focus on your mom, instead of me. And in the fall, we'll be able to honestly say we've seen other people and that we really want to be together. My mom will have calmed down, and we'll be just the same as we were before."

I shook my head. "We won't. *I'll* never be the same again, so I don't know how you think *we* could be. And when you come home in August, you won't come back to *me*." I was proud of myself for sounding so strong when I felt so shattered.

He was quiet for a minute, and then he hurt me even more by saying, "I'm not like your father, Ashley."

The fact that he knew me so well and knew exactly how much my parents' divorce still affected me after so many years made everything worse, so I hurt him back.

"No, you're not," I retorted. "At least when he left my mom and me, he did it for his own reasons and not because his *mommy* told him to. Have a nice summer."

I got up, but he didn't follow.

"I'll still be there for you when I get back," he called out. "I do love you, Ashley – this summer will prove it."

I hated that he got the last word, but more than that, I worried that if I couldn't make a relationship with the perfect guy last, maybe *I* was like *my mother*.

# CHAPTER 3

When I took off from the hill – and from Brandon – I didn't exactly know where I was going, but as I walked, I found myself heading for my best friend Caitlyn's house. It was still early evening, but I sent her a text message to make sure she was home. I didn't have my bike, and I didn't have the strength to walk all the way over there for nothing.

> Can I come over?

>> Yes!!! Y Rn't U with B?

> Tell u when I get there.

I knew that Caitlyn would understand – she'd just broken up with Tyler, a guy she thought she loved but who'd turned out to be a real jerk. I hadn't recognized it at first when she was having problems with him because I'd been so caught up in my own relationship with Brandon. I still felt guilty about it. However, I'd done my best to comfort her and to listen when I realized my mistake, and she finally found the courage to dump him. Now I found myself looking for the same kind of sympathy.

"Brandon's gone," I said when we'd settled in her basement bedroom and she asked again why I wasn't out with him.

She was confused, thinking I meant that he'd already left for canoe camp.

"Already? I thought you guys were still going to have tonight together."

"No – I mean *really* gone – not just to camp, but out of my life," I confessed in a quivering voice, my body shaking with the effort of willing away tears. "He said he wants to 'take a break.'"

"Oh Ashley – I'm so sorry!" Caitlyn hugged me, but she knew me well enough not to press for more details. "He's been such a big part of your life for so long."

"I really thought we were going to be together forever," I said.

She nodded and took my hand. "So did I. Still – 'a break' means there's still the possibility of getting back together ... it doesn't have to be a *permanent* break, right?"

"No," I said, decisively. "I told him he couldn't just decide when he wants to be with me and when he doesn't. It isn't fair." I blotted the beginnings of tears before they could start rolling down my cheeks, and I raised my eyes toward the ceiling. I'd read years ago that rolling your eyes upward makes it physically impossible for tears to form. Crossing your eyes works the same way, but it freaks out your teachers or classmates a lot more than a good upward eye-roll will.

"I am not going to cry over this!" I said, after I'd filled her in on all the details. Then I lowered my eyes and took a deep breath to steady myself.

Nobody knows it, but I used to cry all the time. When I was little, I would just go to bed and cry before going to sleep. I know it was probably a result of my parents' divorce and everything that went before that, but at the time I couldn't have really told you why. Even now, it's hard for me to say exactly. I just know that eventually it stopped, and I didn't want to go there again. So I wouldn't let it start. Not now.

"What's so bad about having a good cry?" Caitlyn asked. "I mean, I think an unexpected break-up after two years justifies some tears."

"I don't think as clearly when I let my emotions take over," I said, still breathing slowly and working hard to control my voice. "I'm already starting to wonder whether we'd just be on 'a break,' instead of permanently broken up if I'd been able to control my anger back on the hill with Brandon."

I looked around her room and saw so many reminders of *her* ex: the paint color they'd put up together, the goldfish he'd given her, the self-portrait – full of anger and pain, and strangely enough, hope – that she'd done right after their break-up.

She let me continue. "But then again, maybe I need to control things *less* … I'm such a neat-freak that I don't even have any big reminders of Brandon on my walls," I blubbered.

"At least you don't have any big reminders of him on your body, either," she said with a half smile. At first I thought she might be referring to the bruises her abusive ex had given her, but then I saw she was pointing to the belly-ring he'd

19

pressured her into getting. At that point, I knew that she was encouraging me to go easier on myself.

"Yeah," I said as I smiled back, as much as I could, and then my voice cracked. "Do you think *I* was being selfish, not agreeing to 'just date,' since we would have been separated all summer anyway? It could have worked out ... he would have been happier that way. His mom would have been okay with it. Why couldn't *I* make myself okay with it?"

"Because as hard as you try," Caitlyn said, "you can't always make everyone happy. And if he doesn't want to go out with you exclusively anymore, then he doesn't *deserve* you anymore," she said. "So *never settle.*"

\* \* \*

My mom was already asleep by the time I got home from Caitlyn's. I was relieved because I didn't want to talk about it any more. Part of me wished I had been staying at my dad's that night – not because I would have talked to him about it, but because at least then I could have been comforted by my Golden Retriever, Daphne.

Daphne is almost twelve years old. She was a "gift" I got when my parents divorced, supposedly because my dad was worried about me being a "lonely only child." But I also suspect Daphne might have been a bit of a bribe because my mom is allergic to dogs – so I'd never been able to have one when she lived with us. As a four-year-old, I'd originally wanted to call the dog *Daffy*, like the duck, but even though the dog was going to live at my dad's place, my mom thought *Daffy* was a silly name for a dog. She talked me into changing it to Daphne.

Daphne loved Brandon. In the beginning, when Brandon and I were shyer with each other, walking her was one thing we could always do together without any awkwardness.

My cell phone buzzed as I changed into my pyjamas. I checked it and saw that Brandon had sent me a text message.

I'm worried about u. Call me!

I deleted it, crawled into bed, and, for the first time in years, cried myself to sleep.

# CHAPTER 4

"So, did you and Brandon say your goodbyes last night?" my mom asked me over breakfast the next morning.

"Yes." I knew she could tell I'd been crying, but I'm sure she thought it was because he was going away to camp without me. Even though part of me was tempted to pretend nothing was wrong, my appearance was already giving me away. Sometimes, I give myself secret nicknames, according to how I'm feeling or what I'm doing – the way they name *Barbie* dolls. Caitlyn once jokingly called me "Overachiever Ashley," but most of time, in my own mind, I felt like "Average Ashley." Today, I was "Puffy-Eyed Ashley."

"Oh, honey," Mom said, smoothing my hair. "I know you'll miss him, but it's just for the summer."

I wasn't sure I was ready, but I decided to spill it. "It's not for the summer – it's forever. Brandon and I broke up."

"What? You broke up?" She took her hand off my hair mid-smooth and sat down, frowning, across from me. "Why?"

"He said we needed to see other people over the summer, but I wouldn't agree to that." My voice was strong again, but my insides felt exhausted and weak, like after I've had the stomach flu.

She studied my face and considered my words before choosing her own words very carefully. "You don't really want to talk about it right now, do you?"

I shook my head, knowing *she* didn't really want to talk about it either because she's a very private person. She always figures everyone else wants to be left alone, like her.

"Let me know if you do," she said. "And look, take this time to be single and to enjoy yourself."

I thought that was a funny comment for my mom to make. *She* doesn't seem to enjoy herself whether she's single *or* part of a couple. Since breaking up with my dad, my mom has been married and divorced two other times. Her second marriage, to Rob, was very brief. She told me once that even though she thought she loved him, it was really just a crush. When the crush wore off, she knew she couldn't stay with him forever, so it seemed better to just end it quickly – before *I* got more attached to him. I haven't seen him since I was little, but he still sends us birthday and Christmas cards.

She got married for the third time, to Greg, when I was ten, and that one lasted two years. He was a little bit younger than her, and they talked about having more kids together because he wanted a big family. But he didn't take his job very seriously, and my mom thought he should be applying for jobs with "greater responsibility." They fought over it a lot, and she finally decided that he didn't have enough ambition.

We never really talked about either of the divorces. Whenever I had tried to bring it up, she'd always just said something like, "We can do better." And maybe she was right – but I'd hoped she would take her own advice and figure it out *before* she got married yet again.

And then, this past April, she discovered that she had breast cancer. In true "Silent Mom" fashion (as I'd come to know it), she'd already found the lump, had it checked and biopsied, and booked her surgery before I knew anything *was* bothering her. Not that I even knew for sure that it was bothering her, because, as always, she said little and admitted almost nothing.

Honestly, I'm not even certain that she would have *ever* told me about the cancer if she could have avoided it, but the surgery was booked during a period when I would have been living at her house. She almost never switches custody with my dad, so she had to explain to both of us where she was going and what was happening.

After the surgery, she started radiation, which was supposed to prevent any spreading or recurrence of the disease. I wanted to tell her that I thought she was brave, but she changed the subject every time I brought that up, too.

So really, because *she* doesn't share her feelings easily, I wasn't surprised when she had so little to say about my break-up with Brandon.

Because Mom tends to *show* that she cares more than she talks about it, I knew she was trying to be supportive when she offered me a ride to the animal shelter that day.

"If you don't feel like taking your bike, I could drop you off," she suggested.

"Thanks, but I'm hoping the exercise will help me clear my head a little," I said.

In my own mind, I was still trying to figure out what had happened. Had Brandon broken up with me? Or had *I* done the breaking up when I refused his new terms? Why did it matter so much to me who'd done it?

I was glad I'd be working that day, since doing something useful would help me take my mind off of Brandon. Still, once I got to the shelter, I found myself rehashing everything and trying to sort out my feelings as I walked the dogs.

*I didn't want to give in and "just date" Brandon*, I thought as Tipper, the German Shepherd, peed on a lamppost. "We were together for a long time," I told the dog. "I don't see how you can go backward, from totally understanding each other and intense making out to 'just dating.' Caitlyn's right. I deserve more than that."

*But maybe I overreacted*, I thought, as J.R., the Jack Russell Terrier, followed me around the yard while I picked up dog poop. *I mean, it's not as if he was going to be around all summer anyway. I could have just gone along with it and let his mom cool down ...*

J.R. circled me, barking. I swung him up gently over my shoulder and whispered in his ear.

"Why can't I just make a decision and stick to it anymore, J.R.? I work hard and I try to be a good person and make mature choices, but suddenly, none of that seems to matter. It really bugs me because I do *not* want to turn into 'that girl' who breaks up with someone and never gets over it."

He snuggled in closer and put his head down. "You know what it's like to get dumped, don't you, buddy?" I asked him. A family had brought him into the shelter because they didn't have time for him. I tried to reassure him the way my mom did the few times she talked about her divorces: "Don't you worry – we can do better."

I hoped he believed me, because I wasn't as sure of myself as I made it sound.

Walking the dogs, hosing out their pens, and cleaning the cats' litter boxes at the shelter made me feel productive again as well as a little less sorry for myself.

When I'd finished at the shelter, I hopped on my bike and headed over to my dad's. The custodial arrangement is "joint," so my parents each get equal time with me. I change houses every fourth day, which seemed like a good idea on paper, but sometimes it feels as if I don't actually live anywhere.

I think the going back and forth between houses might be another part of what makes me such an organized person. I have to know where things are so I don't forget them at the wrong house, and I just feel better if things are set up in a similar way at both places. I like my bed facing the window with my night table on the right. I keep duplicates of basic stuff like underwear and toiletries at both houses so I don't have to drag them around with me, but it's hard with school books and my favorite clothes, so I always end up having to bring a few things back and forth. When that happens, I make sure to unpack my bags and use the closet and the dresser drawers, because I want to feel like I'm *at home* – not visiting – wherever I am.

As soon as I arrived, I gave Daphne a big hug hello. "Brandon left us," I whispered into her neck, and I was comforted when she nuzzled me back in her familiar way. Immediately, I found myself covered in yellow dog fur. Even if I hadn't hugged her, it would have been all over me eventually because my dad lets her sleep on the couch. His house isn't dirty or gross, but it's much more relaxed and comfortable than my mom's house. Mom's place is neater and tidier and more controlled, like her. *Everything* has a spot, and she can't sit down and relax until things are back where they belong. Not that she sits down to relax very often. My dad jokes that nobody ever died wishing they'd done more housework; my mom jokes that she'd die of embarrassment if someone came over and her place wasn't clean. When it comes to organization, I'm more like my mom, but I don't know if it's hereditary or if it's just from living with her.

Daphne followed me around while I got myself settled and straightened up some stuff in the main part of the house. Dad had a lot of pictures of me on display, at all different stages of my life. There was one of Brandon and me dressed up as a bride and groom for Halloween the year before. When he'd seen us, Dad had joked that maybe, when the time came for us to actually get married, we could save him some money by eloping because he already had the pictures anyway.

I took that photo off the shelf along with a couple of other recent ones from the spring dance and shoved them into a drawer so I wouldn't have to be reminded of Brandon.

Then I went out to the backyard with Daphne and played fetch in the sun until we were both exhausted. Dad had texted me earlier to say we'd be going out for dinner, and although I always felt a bit guilty going out and leaving Daphne on the nights we could have spent time together, it was easier when I knew she was good and tired.

"Hey, sunshine!" my dad called from the back door when he got in after work. "Are you ready to go? We have a reservation downtown in twenty minutes."

A "reservation" obviously meant we weren't going out to our usual Italian place for our favorite chicken penne. It made me suspicious that my mom had already filled him in on my "news" and that he was trying to cheer me up.

"I don't know – I'm not really dressed for a fancy restaurant," I said, looking down at my shorts and sandals. "Casual Ashley" didn't usually have a place at my mom's house, but "Styling Ashley" tended to make my dad worry that I was overly concerned about appearances – the way my mom was. Even though my parents couldn't tell me what to wear, I usually ended up dressed more casually at my dad's house.

Dad smiled and hugged me tight. "You look lovely, as always. Let's go – there's someone in the car I want you to meet."

That "someone" was about to change my whole summer.

# CHAPTER 5

Even before we got up to the car, I could see that there was a woman in the front seat. I turned to raise my eyebrows at my dad. He grinned back at me. My mom had already been remarried twice, but as far as I knew, my dad hadn't dated anyone "special" since my mom, and I only remembered him introducing me to one other girlfriend. So I knew there had to be something different about this one.

"Ashley," he said as I got into the car, "*this* is Gabriella. Gabriella, my daughter, Ashley."

The woman turned around and reached between the seats to shake my hand. "It's wonderful to meet you, Ashley. Your dad brags about you and your accomplishments all the time."

"Hi, it's nice to meet to you, too," I said, intrigued, but slightly annoyed that I hadn't been prepped for this meeting the way she obviously had been. My first impression was that she was someone who took pride in her appearance, like my mom. Her teeth were bright white and contrasted sharply with her large dark sunglasses. She had light-blonde hair that hung loosely around her face.

"All right, ladies, dinner awaits!" Dad announced gleefully as he got in the driver's seat. His obvious joy made me smile for real for the first time in the twenty-four hours since The Break-Up. "I can't wait," Gabriella said to him, turning back to face frontward. "Do you two mind if I put some music on?" she asked as she began flipping through my dad's MP3 tunes. "There's just something about upbeat music and summertime driving that go so well together."

My dad and I agreed, and she chose an eighties song, cranked up the volume, and jerked her head along with the beat while at the same time belting out the occasional lyric. My dad kept grinning and glancing from the road, to her. He was totally smitten. I hoped, for his sake, that Gabriella already felt the same way about him, because if she didn't, she was going to think he was a total dork.

It was hard to talk with the music on, so I spent most of the ride checking Gabriella out from the backseat as subtly as possible. She was more dressed up than I was, which kind of made me wish I hadn't listened to my dad when he'd said my shorts were okay. Her perfume was light and lemony – not heavy and flowery, like I would have expected from someone her age.

Once we'd been seated at the restaurant, with the two of them side by side and me across from my dad, I saw that despite how young Gabriella's trendy clothes made her seem, she was probably in her mid-forties, about the same age as my mom. It was hard to say for certain, though. My mom was always worrying about the "laugh lines" (aka: wrinkles) around her mouth, but Gabriella didn't have any, and the skin around her deep blue eyes didn't crinkle up at all when she smiled. I wondered if that was why it seemed as if her gaze was so intense, or whether she was sizing me up, the way I'd been evaluating her. It made me feel a little bit guilty for looking her over so carefully.

Gabriella didn't wait for my dad to break the ice any further – she started right in with conversation as soon as our orders had been taken. "So, your dad tells me you work at an animal shelter in town?"

"Not *work*, exactly – I volunteer. I want to go to veterinary college eventually, so I'm hoping the experience will teach me about animal care *and* help my applications," I explained.

"That's so sweet! I love dogs, and Daphne is just adorable."

I don't know why it hadn't occurred to me before that she would have been to Dad's house (I mean, really, they *were* dating!) – maybe it was just because he hadn't mentioned that he'd been seeing anyone special. In any case, it felt weird to suddenly learn that this stranger was already so familiar with my Daphne ... and my dad ... and yet, I was just meeting her for the first time. It was sort of like starting a movie halfway through and trying to catch up without bugging everyone else for the details about what you've already missed.

"Yeah – Daphne's pretty special," I said. "We have other kinds of animals at the shelter, too, though – not just dogs. There are always a lot of cats, and we usually have a rabbit or two – especially after Easter – and right now we have some hamsters and rats – "

"Rats? You take *rats* at an animal shelter?"

I didn't know why that was such a big deal. I looked at my dad, as if for an explanation, and he took her hand in his as he waited for me to continue.

"Yes," I answered. "We have *pet* rats – we'll take pretty much any animal that people have changed their minds about and don't want anymore."

Thinking about people changing their minds reminded me again of Brandon, and I noticed the tight feeling returning to my stomach. I had planned to talk to my dad about him over dinner, but I didn't want to get into the details of The Break-Up in front of Gabriella, who was still essentially a stranger to me.

"So, anyway," I continued after pausing for a sip of water, "we do get rats in as pets that need to be re-homed, but then we also bring in feeder rats for the Python and the Anaconda – which is a bit unfair, I guess."

She looked as if I'd offered up one of the rats for *her* dinner. "Ooh, I can't stand snakes. Who would want a pet *snake*?"

"They're not my favorite, either," I admitted, "but 'beauty is in the eye of the beholder,' right? Who's to say that a kitten is cuter than a snake?"

"*Me*, that's who." She leaned forward so far that I inadvertently backed up a bit. "I run a modeling school. The Gabriella McCullough School of Modeling? Downtown?"

I *had* heard of it, but I was surprised that it belonged to her. Some of the girls from school took classes there, and I'd seen the ads in the paper, but I'd always pictured a very prim and proper old lady running it – not the enthusiastic young-ish woman across from me.

She continued. "I *know* cute, and you, Ashley, *you* are so much more than cute – *you* are *stunning.*" She turned back to my father and said it again, with an emphasis on every word as if she couldn't believe it. "Your daughter is just stunning!"

It felt like a bizarre flashback to the prior night and Brandon's "you're totally gorgeous" speech right before he dumped me. I held my breath and braced myself for a new bombshell, like, "You're so beautiful, I can't wait for you to be a bridesmaid when I marry your father!"

Dad smiled even wider than before. "Well, *I've* always thought so…" he said.

"Um, thank you," I replied, embarrassed, to both of them. I wished I'd sat beside Gabriella, instead of across from the two of them, because then it would have been easier to avoid her intense gaze.

"Gabriella said it as soon as she saw your pictures at my place, Ashley," Dad interjected with obvious pride. "Her exact words were: 'This girl is model material and I need talk to her about getting into the industry.'"

I laughed nervously, uncomfortable with such praise. Even though my mom always expected me to look my best, she still emphasized my accomplishments over my appearances. And as for my dad, well, he was the guy who'd said it

33

would be okay for me to come to dinner at a sit-down restaurant with his new girlfriend *in my shorts and sandals*. He seemed to know beautiful women when he saw them – like my mom and Gabriella – but he never talked about their appearances, or mine.

"I do want to get you involved in modeling, Ashley," Gabriella enthused. "That's why I pushed your father to let me meet you tonight, in person – though I'm sure we would have met soon, anyway," she said as she smiled up at him and squeezed his hand.

"You happen to have *the* hottest look in fashion right now," she said seriously, looking at me again. "There are certain things that never go out of style in the modeling industry: height, facial symmetry, and flawless skin – you've got all of that. You've also got the current weight-to-height ratios and unusual coloring with your naturally dark hair and green eyes. That makes you unique and very marketable. You *should* be a model."

I was flattered that she'd ask. The girls I knew who had taken classes at Gabriella's modeling school did fashion shows at the mall sometimes. I knew I was tall enough, but I hadn't ever really thought of myself as being model material.

"That might be kind of fun," I told her. "But I'd have to work it around my volunteer work at the shelter … and maybe around the days I'm staying with my mom, depending on how she feels about it. When would the classes be?"

Gabriella looked up at my dad with a questioning look on her face.

"Sweetheart, Gabriella used to model professionally herself, and she still has a lot of high-profile contacts in the industry. She's not suggesting that you take classes from her. She wants to help you get into the modeling business *professionally*. Magazines, high-end fashion shows – all of it."

Gabriella couldn't let him finish without jumping back into the conversation. "Ashley, you seem very confident, mature, and well-spoken. If you're willing to work with me, I really, really, think you could be quite successful as a professional model." She seemed sincere and sure of what she was saying. I wished I could believe her more easily.

"I know it's a lot to take in, Ashley," my dad continued, "and I wasn't sure about it when she first brought it up, but Gabriella's convinced me that this could really provide you with some wonderful opportunities. You could travel, and it would give you the chance to earn quite a bit of money for university or for a house someday in the future. I think you should consider it."

In my mind, I quickly ran through all the things I knew – or thought I knew – about modeling. I closed my eyes and considered the stiff competition and the slim chances of actually achieving any measure of success. I thought about the possibility of public failure, and I felt myself tensing up again. But then I looked at their expectant faces and felt as if I didn't have any choice but to try.

"Tell me what I'd have to do," I said.

# CHAPTER 6

Hearing me ask what I had to do to succeed in modeling made Gabriella even more animated, and for a second I thought she might leap across the table in her enthusiasm. She wasted no time explaining how we should proceed. "I'm thinking our best shot right now is the National Modeling Convention," she said. "It's just a few weeks away. It's by invitation only, but we can still get you registered."

Suddenly, I was alert and energized by the idea of modeling, and the fact that the convention – my *best shot* – was "just a few weeks away" both thrilled and terrified me. I was glad it wasn't going to be a long drawn-out summer of taking modeling classes, because even though I always weigh my options, once I decide to do something, I don't like to wait. At the same time, I didn't yet know what I'd be jumping into, or whether "a few weeks" would be enough time to prepare.

"What exactly is a modeling – *convention* – did you say?"

"It's a giant casting call, really. A showcase for up-and-coming talent. Local agencies like us send models to gain experience under pressure. Bigger, international agencies send in their scouts to find fresh faces. It's win-win for everyone."

"So what would Ashley have to do at this convention?" my dad asked. I'd been so caught up in what Gabriella was saying that I'd almost forgotten he was there.

Even though she was answering my dad's question, she addressed me when she spoke, as if I was her equal, rather than just her date's teenaged daughter. "You'd perform in runway and photography categories and maybe some acting – in case you want to pursue commercials – but you'd have free time, too, and the chance to meet with some very prestigious agencies. It's a great opportunity, and," she added "it's a lot of fun."

"So, it's like a beauty pageant?" I asked.

"Not exactly," she explained. "There are some titles and contracts awarded, but there's not one overall winner. You wouldn't really be competing *against* other people so much as creating opportunities for yourself."

"Okay, but what kind of opportunities are we talking about?"

"Well, last year we sent Lia Geniene to the convention – you may know her – the blond from the Café Divine commercials? She got the contract for those ads through an agent she met at the convention, and she's already paid a semester's tuition at university through that campaign."

My dad was still smiling, but now he seemed to have that faraway look that he gets on my birthday or whenever I dress up for a special occasion.

"Wow, it sounds very cool," I said. "And Dad's obviously okay with this," – he nodded vigorously – "but I'm going to have to run this by my mom."

"Of course," Gabriella said as she smiled in a way that I found reassuring. "Please tell her to call me if she has any questions at all."

Like *that* was going to happen. My mom can be super-controlling and occasionally overprotective, but I didn't imagine that she'd be jumping at the chance to call Dad's new girlfriend.

"Her mother ought to be flattered – Ashley looks just like her," my dad said. I turned quickly to check Gabriella's expression, but it was neutral. She obviously didn't feel threatened by the mention of dad's ex-wife. I decided that I liked that about her.

"So, assuming we're going to proceed, you'll need a portfolio. We don't have much time to pull something together before the convention. I can arrange a photo shoot for you – at a very minimal cost – with a professional photographer if you're ready to get started."

I was *so* ready that I needed to tell someone else, right away. Before the food came, I excused myself to go wash my hands, but I really just wanted to share my news with Caitlyn. I decided it was better to text than call, because if I phoned, there was still a good possibility that Gabriella could come into the bathroom and overhear me. I didn't want her to think I was immature.

3 thngs

Dad + new gf

gf = model agent

Agent + me = !!!

L8r

It was cryptic, but I didn't want to take forever keying in the details, and I knew Caitlyn would get the gist of it. I hoped it didn't sound conceited, like I was bragging, but I was just so happy to have a distraction from Brandon and I had to share the good news with her.

The distraction was short-lived. When I got back to the table, Dad and Gabriella were holding hands and kind of nuzzling into each other, the way Brandon and I used to. I know it's unfair, but I always think that a *high school* couple in love looks cute, but a *grown-up* couple in love looks kind of ridiculous. Seeing my dad and Gabriella like that did make me ache a little bit inside, though, missing Brandon. Right up until the day before, he would have been the first one I would have told this news to. I started to imagine how he would have reacted. I pictured him pulling me into his "happy dance," the way he had when he'd found out he'd been selected as a counsellor at the camp.

But now? I did believe he'd still be happy for me. And a little part of me kind of hoped he'd have one of those pangs of regret, like in the lottery commercials where people realize their numbers won and they forgot to play. Either way, I had a new focus and a new goal.

"Sorry, sweetie, I still haven't had a chance to catch up with you," Dad apologized when I sat down again. He glanced at me, then back at Gabriella.

She understood his look. "I think I'll just excuse myself

for a minute, if you don't mind," she said, getting up and heading for the washroom. I wondered if she had someone she needed to text, too.

When she was out of earshot, I took a deep breath and shared my other news with my dad.

"I broke up with Brandon last night. But I don't want to talk about it."

In that instant, I noticed a subtle change in how it felt to say the words "I broke up with Brandon" instead of "We broke up" or "He dumped me." I sat up straighter and decided that whether or not it had been mutual (and "*Confused Ashley*" still wasn't actually sure) that was the only way I was ever going to describe it from that point on.

Dad looked wounded, and I knew he felt as if he'd lost something, too. "Okay," he said slowly. "So, I know you said you don't want to talk about it, but could you expand – even just *a little bit* – for an old guy like me?"

I knew that having to "expand on it," whether or not I wanted to, was my fault for even mentioning it at all. The say-it-then-drop-it newsflash worked on my mom, but I should have known Dad wouldn't let it go. I rolled my eyes up, which stopped me from getting emotional again, and, I hoped, would also give the impression that I didn't really care.

"I broke up with Brandon."

"I got *that*, Ashley. This is the part where you *expaaaaand* on the details." My dad tried a different tactic, giving up on "Concerned Father" and instead playing "Comic Sidekick." He dragged out the word "expand" when he said it in a way that made him look and sound like a cartoon character. I loved him for trying to make me laugh, even though I wouldn't give in and do it.

I shrugged. "We wanted different things. He was going to be gone all summer anyway."

"So I'm not going to have to pay for that big wedding after all?" he joked again, still trying to coax a giggle out of me.

"No, but you might have to pay for a hot-fudge brownie sundae," I said hopefully. "Because we were together a long time, and I *am* sad." I used a tone that I hoped sounded funny, even though I wasn't quite sure I could pull it off. Then I added, "And the more painful memories you bring up, the less ice cream I'm going to share with you, so if I were you, I'd drop the whole subject."

Dad took the hint and excused me from any further discussion of Brandon.

"I don't often work with girls who aren't afraid to celebrate with a little ice cream," Gabriella said upon returning from the washroom just as I'd ordered the sundae.

I hadn't planned it to be a celebration, but surprisingly, with the fresh challenge of modeling before me, dessert on the way, and my dad being goofier than usual, I managed to stop thinking about Brandon for most of the evening.

\* \* \*

When we got home that night, I called my mom to tell her the news. She wasn't quite as excited as my dad had thought she'd be.

"What do you mean your dad's new girlfriend used to be a model?" she asked.

"That's not the important part, Mom," I said quickly, wanting to finish my story before she interrupted again. "She runs a modeling school now, and she thinks *I* should model."

I could hear the concern in her voice, even though she was trying to be supportive. "You know I'd never discourage you from trying something new," she said. "As long as you understand how modeling schools work – you know, they give you a bunch of promises, and then they get you to take a class. And then another."

"That's what I thought she meant at first, too, Mom, but she's not talking about classes at her school – she wants to help me get into modeling *professionally*. She says I've got the height, the look, everything, and she's certain I could get paying modeling jobs."

She paused for a minute. "Okay. Start again at the beginning and tell me everything. What were you wearing when you met her?"

"Nothing special – just shorts and sandals."

"Mmm. *I* wouldn't have let you go to dinner like that. I'm glad *she* saw past it, but this is exactly why I always say you should make an effort to look your best all the time, Ashley. You just never know who you're going to run into."

I waited while she continued, wondering whether she was right. I know my mom was careful to get dressed and do her hair and make-up the same as always while undergoing the radiation for her cancer. She *said* it made her feel better not to walk around looking sick. But I know that for me, sometimes, just wearing a loose pair of pyjama bottoms is comfortable. And Gabriella obviously hadn't been worried about what I was wearing.

"Anyway," I continued, "she thinks I can move out of the local market and into some real money-making opportunities if I make the right contacts at the convention. Last year, that girl in the Café Divine ads got discovered there," I explained.

"Oh, I'm sure there are occasional success stories to keep the businesses floating. And if you want to try it, I think you should. Just don't let yourself get side-tracked by it, that's all."

"Side-tracked from what?"

"Your studies."

"Mom, it's summer! I don't have any 'studies,' remember? And when have I ever been 'side-tracked?'"

"I mean in the future – after high school – I'd hate to see you give up your dreams of being a vet to pursue success in modeling when it's likely to be so … unattainable," she said.

"You always said I could be anything I wanted," I challenged. "And it's not unattainable if I'm being *asked* to try it."

"You're right," she softened. "I shouldn't be giving you such a hard time. I just want what's best for you."

I know my mom cares a lot, and that it's always the reason behind her advice and cautions, but sometimes I think that what's "best" for me would be for her to just trust that she's raised me to be responsible, and to let me do things my own way occasionally – even if I *am* doing it in shorts and sandals.

After I hung up with my mom, I called Caitlyn and filled *her* in on all the same details. She Googled Gabriella's name while we talked.

"Whoa," she said with obvious surprise. "Did Gabriella tell you about all the cool things she's done?"

"I don't know – what do you mean by cool? She told me she used to be a model and that last year she sent Lia Geniene – from the Café Divine ads – to the convention ..." I felt a bit guilty just then, realizing that most of our dinner had been spent talking about me – *my* interests, *my* potential, and *my* boyfriend – or lack thereof. I hadn't actually taken the time get to know my dad's new girlfriend, and I knew I would have hated it if anyone had done that to me.

"Well, it says here that she used to be a model, and they show her on some magazine covers and stuff ... you should look this up when you get the chance. It seems like she made a pretty good living at it before opening her modeling school, which she only runs for part of the year."

"What does she do for the rest of the year?" I asked.

"She travels, she competed in a marathon across the Sahara Desert last fall, she's served on judges' panels for that modeling convention a couple of times, she does charity work at the hospital with a program called 'Looking good, Looking up' for cancer patients. Oh my gosh, Ashley, she sounds amazing."

"So I wonder why she lives here, instead of a bigger city?" I asked. "And why doesn't she model anymore?"

"I guess you'll have to ask her that yourself. So what happens next for you?"

"I'm going to meet her again tomorrow at her office, to talk about a few more things. And then she's going to arrange a photo shoot so I'll have a portfolio before the convention."

I wasn't "the girl with the hot boyfriend" anymore, but Gabriella hadn't known me as her anyway, and she'd still seen something special in me. I hoped that maybe when I got the photos taken, I'd be able to see it, too.

# CHAPTER 7

The next day, I rushed through my chores at the shelter in anticipation of the follow-up with Gabriella.

I was surprised to find myself feeling anxious about the second meeting with her. There was no reason why she should have changed her mind, but now that I'd told Caitlyn and my mom about it, I was starting to worry that maybe things wouldn't work out as easily as Gabriella had suggested they might.

"Ashley!" she kissed each of my cheeks lightly, as if we were old friends, when I got to the office. I wondered whether she did this with all of her models, or whether it was a special greeting for me as her boyfriend's daughter.

The modeling school was in an old Victorian-style house that had been converted into a business. I guessed that her office might once have been a dining room or a parlor, because it was at the front of the house and it had big bay windows all around. The furniture had a polished antique look, as if it was new but was made in an old-fashioned style. She had a desk, a sideboard, and a couple of upholstered chairs. One wall of the office was covered in narrow shelving that held small photo albums, and on the front of each album was a photogenic face.

"Your portfolio will be something like these," she said as she waved her arm in a graceful sweep in front of the shelves. "We'll get a few great shots at your photo shoot, which I've booked for Monday, and then when you start working professionally, we'll add that work to your book."

"So people who want models look at these books?" I asked, picking up one with a hot-looking guy on the cover.

"Sometimes," she acknowledged. "Having the portfolios here also helps me see at a glance who I might want to send out for a job. Say if a client called looking for a man in his twenties, with dark hair – I could have these gentlemen, here," she gestured to one section of albums, "meet with the client directly – taking their own copy of their portfolio with them, of course."

"Will my pictures really look as beautiful as these?" I asked, hoping the question didn't suggest any insecurity.

"*Better*," she assured me. "I've seen the snapshots at your dad's place – you're quite photogenic all on your own, so I'm certain that with professional styling and make-up, we'll get something really special."

"So today is all about preparation," she continued as she pulled a tape measure out of her desk drawer. "I need to get your measurements, and then I'll have some clothes sent over to the studio for the shoot. We don't usually provide the outfits, but I have some ideas about how these shots should look, so I'm going to call in a favor with a boutique owner I know."

"What kind of 'look' are we going for?" I asked, raising my arms so she could measure my waist.

"For the portfolio, we're actually going for three very *different* looks. But I did want to talk to you about your basic appearance. I'm thinking we could *enhance* your natural beauty with a trip to the right salon ... we'll get the ends of your hair trimmed up *now* so it's fresh for the photos, but softened up by the convention."

It struck me as funny how Gabriella, in so many ways, reminded me of my mother – she was beautiful and successful, and she also seemed to have strong opinions. And yet, while Mom was always saying "you" should do this or "you" should do that, with Gabriella, everything was "we."

* * *

Because of my appointment at the spa, I had to rush through my chores at the shelter for the second day in a row. As always, it made me feel guilty to leave all of my charges in their pens while I went off to get pampered.

"The right salon" turned out to be a high-end spa in town that Gabriella regularly went to herself. She'd already spoken to my dad about leaving his credit card information, and she'd booked me an appointment. I didn't yet know what she actually had in store for me.

When I got to the salon, I learned that Gabriella had scheduled me in with her own hair stylist, Kyle. "So we'll be adding a variety of soft highlights?" he looked at me questioningly in the mirror.

"Umm … I don't think so – we didn't actually discuss *dyeing* my hair. I think I'm just here to get it trimmed a bit."

"Ooh. That's not what my notes say – but I didn't talk to Gabriella directly. Let me double-check with reception," he went off to confirm that color was, in fact, part of the plan. I studied myself in the mirror while he was gone, trying to figure out how highlights would look and whether there was anything else I needed to do before my portfolio pictures on Monday. I was just thinking that maybe I should get some tooth whitener when he returned with a cordless phone in hand.

"I have Gabriella on the line," he said, passing the telephone to me.

"Hello?"

"Hi – Ashley? Listen – I know we only talked about shaping your hair, but I was thinking about it last night, and it occurred to me that as lovely as your natural color is, a few well-placed highlights would really just make your eyes pop, so I've explained to Kyle what it is I'm going for and he's going to look after you – okay?"

"There's no chance that this is going to go all wrong and make me look like a clown or dry my hair out, right?" I asked hesitantly, feeling my body tense up the way it had that night on the hill. "Because my mom tried highlights a few years ago and they came out orangey on her dark hair. It was kind of like a cheesy tiger-print scarf." Gabriella laughed at the metaphor without recognizing my depth of concern underneath it.

"You're in very capable hands there, Ashley – Kyle's

really the best in town. And, listen, while I've got you on the phone, I've booked you in for a French manicure, as well. We just want to make sure your hands have a really clean look in the close-ups."

"Okay," I told her. "I'll trust your judgment." I handed the phone back to Kyle and hoped my own judgment – in trusting Gabriella – was right.

Caitlyn always says that when I get something in my head, there's no changing my mind. She has no idea how often I actually *do* change my mind, though, when I know that doing so will make other people happier – my mother, or (apparently) Gabriella, for example.

Normally, because I'm such a planner, I would have thought about my hair in great detail and maybe even tried out the highlights in advance on one of those computer programs where you can make yourself over digitally. I felt uneasy about making such an important beauty decision on the spot – but Gabriella was doing so much for me, I didn't want to argue or come across as being high maintenance. And, being newly single, I told myself that altering my appearance – even slightly – might make me feel new *and* improved.

Hours later, I still didn't know if I'd done the right thing.

# CHAPTER 8

"**W**ow! What did they do with my daughter?" my dad asked when he got home from work that afternoon and saw my new "look."

"I think she's still here – but I can understand that you may be blinded by the highlights," I said from the patio table, where Caitlyn and I were eating popsicles and trying to adjust to my new, lighter, and multi-colored hair.

"You know," he continued, "we always *said* you were bright – and now you have the hair to prove it!"

"*Daaa-aad!* I'm still trying to get used to it – and you aren't helping," I moaned as Caitlyn laughed out loud.

"Sorry, sunshine," Dad said as he kissed my formerly dark hair. I was tempted to ask him whether the copper, bronze, and gold highlights tasted metallic at all.

"I didn't realize you were getting so much done," he said. "I was under the impression that my credit card was just taking care of a trim."

"I was, too," I confessed. "But then everyone suggested highlights to 'freshen up my look,' and now ... here I am. 'Glow-Bug Ashley.'"

"They really *do* look gorgeous, Ashley. I'm just not used to seeing you with such light hair, so it kind of threw me off."

"I've been telling her that all afternoon," Caitlyn said. "The contrast really gives it depth."

I looked again in the hand mirror and tried to see myself objectively, without remembering the Ashley I used to be. The effect of the highlights on my hair *was* pretty; the girl in the mirror just wasn't the one I was expecting when I looked.

I devoted the rest of the evening and the next couple of days almost entirely to getting ready for the portfolio shoot. I'd started a small notebook to keep track of the information Gabriella had shared with me so I wouldn't forget anything. She'd already explained to me, for example, that I needed to wear sunscreen applied very evenly – or better yet, stay out of the sun entirely as tan lines would be totally undesirable and hard to fix in my pictures.

I'd also been trying to do a lot of independent research because I have always hated asking for help with anything. Even when I was little, my mom says I spent weeks and weeks tripping over my own feet because I refused to let anyone tie my shoelaces for me, even though I didn't yet have the fine motor skills needed to tie them myself. A lot of kids would have given in after landing on their faces a couple of times, or they would have refused to wear lace-up shoes altogether, but I just kept wearing them and falling down and getting back up until I finally got it all together.

That obstinate part of me didn't want to keep bugging Gabriella, so I was trying to do my own prep work by buying and reading lots of magazines. Researching modeling on the internet was proving more difficult than I'd expected, because every time I typed in "teen models," I ended up with a bunch of disgusting websites advertising "hot young girls." It felt like a waste of time picking through that kind of garbage trying to find legitimate sites, and it bugged me.

On Sunday afternoon, it was time for me to move back to my mom's. Even though her house is close to my dad's, I hadn't yet been over to show her my new look. I was concerned about her reaction.

"Wow! I didn't know you were getting your hair done," she said as she hugged me after my arrival and then stood back to scrutinize me.

"I had my nails done, too," I said, wiggling them up and down to show them off.

She smiled sadly then and seemed disappointed. At first I thought she didn't like my new look, but then she nodded and said, "A little pampering is always a great idea after a break-up. I bet it did you a lot of good. I could have come with you, though, and we could have had a spa day together."

"It just kind of came up at the last minute," I explained, relieved that she approved but surprised by how defeated she looked. "Maybe we can do it another time?"

She tried to smile again for real, but she looked tired and unsure. "Maybe."

My photo shoot was the next day, and my mom had agreed to drive me on her way to work, so she could see what it was all about. But when I came downstairs, in my hoodie and shorts, she looked as if she'd changed her mind.

"What was all that time in the bathroom about? You're not ready!" she exclaimed.

"I was shaving my legs very carefully, and yes, I *am* ready."

"You're going like that?" she asked, appalled, as I put my sandals on. "To have your *picture* taken?"

"This is how I'm supposed to go," I explained, gesturing toward my hair. "Gabriella said I should be *fresh* – make-up free, with clean, dry hair that hasn't got any products in it."

"Are you sure?" She was still eyeing me suspiciously. Never in my memory has my mother left the house without full hair and make-up. And although *I* don't usually wear a *lot* of make-up, she prefers me to be "done" whenever I go out too.

I crossed my arms in front of my chest and hoped she wouldn't notice that I wasn't wearing a bra. Caitlyn had told me that when people pose in the nude for artists, they made sure to wear loose clothing without undergarments. Otherwise they could end up with marks on their skin caused by the elastic. She's never actually drawn a nude, but her friend Conner had taken an art class with some university students who earned money modeling that way. Even though *I* wasn't going to be posing naked, I wanted to be prepared in case there were any strapless or backless outfits in my wardrobe. I had some different styles of bras and underwear with me to wear underneath whatever clothes they had for me, but I wouldn't know what was right until I got there.

All the way to the studio, I imagined it would be posh

and contemporary, like the salon. I'd been expecting a large sign announcing what it was, but once we'd found the address, it turned out to be nothing more than one worn-out door stuck between a couple of old buildings, with a 6x8 sign that had the photographer's name on it. "This isn't exactly the glamorous start I was anticipating," I noted as my mom parked and I unbuckled my seatbelt.

"I'm coming up with you, just for a minute," my mom said.

She hadn't planned on staying. I wasn't surprised, because even when she had radiation every day, she booked it for first thing in the morning and then she would dash back into work as soon as it was finished. Mom had had perfect attendance when she was in high school and she *still* bragged about it. Now that she's a partner in an accounting firm, she is just as committed. Even when she has a cold or the flu, she never misses a day on the job, so it was a matter of personal pride for her to be battling breast cancer without taking off any more time than absolutely necessary. I knew that if she wasn't taking time off for *cancer*, she certainly wasn't going to take it for *me*.

"I'll be okay," I said, knowing she was feeling apprehensive about leaving me alone in a strange place, despite her resolve not to stay.

"I know," she said brusquely. "But I'd like to see it for myself."

Together, we climbed up the steep staircase to the second floor and entered the studio. Once we were inside, the building's age and location made a lot more sense. The old windows were tall and expansive and the floor was hardwood. There were room-dividing screens, large lights on poles, and a number of cameras. It was definitely a studio.

A woman with pink streaks in her black hair met us by the door.

"Ashley?" she asked.

I nodded and said, "Hi.".

"We're doing your make-up over there, in the back corner," she said as she indicated with a flick of her chin in the direction I should take. Then she looked back at my mother. "Are you staying?"

"No," she sighed. "I'd love to, but I have to get to work."

"It's usually easier for the girls without having their parents hanging around anyway," the woman said.

"I can see how it might be, but still," she said as she pouted and bit her bottom lip. For an instant, I wondered whether she might actually change her mind and stay. Then her regular decisiveness returned and she said, "All right, Ashley, do exactly what they tell you, and then do it better." She gave me a little half-wave and headed out.

"Pink Streaks" had already motioned me over to a dressing table and had begun combing out my hair and setting it with hot-rollers, but she hadn't yet said another word to me.

"I'm sorry," I began. "I didn't catch your name?"

"Jordyn," she said, leaning over and looking at me closely from behind in the mirror. "We're going to need to do a little tweezing on those brows. You see here? Where the arch should be?" she pointed to an area under my eyebrows.

"Umm, okay," I said. I looked carefully at my reflection in the mirror, trying to see what she planned on doing to my eyebrows. I thought I kept them fairly well groomed by myself – it wasn't as if I had a uni-brow or anything – but it seemed that I'd missed *something*.

"Do you do the make-up, too? Or just the hair?"

Jordyn was rummaging for something that turned out to be tweezers. "Both. Make-up and hair. I help out with the equipment during the shoot sometimes, too."

I was relieved that she was finally looking at me while she talked, but I still got the impression that she was annoyed to have to be up so early to work on me. She was leaning in close to my face while she tended to my eyebrows, and I could smell her shampoo. It had a fake strawberry scent, like red Jell-O. I was still trying to think of something else to say when the door opened behind me and I heard Gabriella's cheerful voice saying "Good morning."

"Ashley! Jordyn! How are we doing? Your highlights are beautiful, Ashley – I'm so glad we had them done. I had a few extra minutes and I wanted to come over to make sure everything was perfect. I won't kiss you because I don't want to mess up any of Jordyn's work."

"We're just about to start the make-up," Jordyn said, pulling out a spray bottle and a sponge.

"Let me see your manicure," Gabriella said to me.

As my sleeves fell when I lifted my hands to show her, she shrieked.

# CHAPTER 9

"What's that on your arms?" Gabriella asked as she examined the thin red streaks crisscrossing my wrists and forearms.

"Oh. Scratches. We have a litter of kittens at the shelter," I said, wondering why she hadn't noticed them before.

She exhaled with exasperation just as my mother would have done. "Well we can't have you looking all scratched up in the photos." I was embarrassed that I hadn't considered it before, especially when I remembered how it had freaked Brandon out, too.

"Jordyn, can you do anything about them?" Gabriella asked.

"I can try some thick concealer."

"Great," she said to Jordyn. "Work your magic. I want to go check out the clothes I had sent over." Sitting there with my flaws exposed gave me an odd sense of having been disciplined.

Jordyn took out some green concealer and began dabbing it on my scratches.

"Why green?" I asked.

"Because" – now she sounded a little irritated – "the

scratches are mostly red, and green is opposite to red on the color wheel. Complementary colors tone each other down, so when I add flesh-tone concealer on top, it will be that much more effective."

Caitlyn would have known that. "Is this going to work?" I asked, worried.

"I think so," she said.

She finished touching up the scratches, then began again on my face. I could hear Gabriella murmuring in the far corner of the studio, but I couldn't see her in the mirror, and I couldn't turn around.

As Jordyn pulled out a huge brush to stipple powder on my face, I began to sympathize with all the dogs I'd used flea powder on at the shelter. When I accidentally inhaled some powder, it made me cough.

She stood back and waited while I caught my breath, but she didn't apologize.

Gabriella appeared in front of me again and smiled brightly. She seemed to be in a better mood when she looked at my arms. "Good job, Jordyn! Ashley – the clothes I ordered are all here and they're going to look gorgeous on you. I can't stay, but I'll see you later. I'll be sure to tell your father how wonderful you've been to work with. Oh – and remember, keep yourself turned toward the lights while Craig's taking your pictures."

"Your father?" Jordyn asked after Gabriella had left.

"She's dating him," I said.

"Oh." She nodded, but she didn't ask anything else.

I hoped she didn't think I was only there because of the connection.

"So, what's the best thing about being a make-up artist?" I asked, trying to change the subject. "Being able to do it on yourself, too?"

"I guess," she shrugged. "It's a nice challenge, usually. You wouldn't believe some of the faces I have to work on. Yours isn't too bad, actually."

*There's a quote that will get me modeling jobs*, I thought. Her face *"isn't too bad."* Wow. Three little words every girl wants to hear! Oddly enough, deciding that my face "isn't too bad" seemed to make Jordyn chattier.

"You have no idea," she said dryly, "what most models look like before we get in there with make-up, lighting, and digital re-touching. Some of the most famous girls have the worst under-eye circles. Or over-plucked eyebrows that I have to draw back *on*. At least you came in with thicker ones – that's easier to fix. I see a lot of skinny lips, too. We do a lot to plump out lips and make them look fuller."

"So, it actually doesn't matter how we come in?" I questioned. "Because really, it sounds like you can change anyone anyway – "

"Oh no – I didn't mean that just anyone could model," she smiled, finally, and I realized that she was just a bit insecure herself. "You really do need to have good bone structure, height – all the things Gabriella probably already talked to you about. I can enhance your features with make-up, but I can't invent them. Close your eyes for a minute."

"Okay." I squirmed in my seat and tried to focus on what she was saying and not on what a screw-up I felt like. I'd already read a lot of stuff online and in magazines about how sometimes the girl you think is totally gorgeous ends up not being photogenic at all and doesn't come across as pretty on camera. But others, who look very plain and ordinary, just sparkle in photographs. I was trying to figure out which category I fit into, though I wasn't sure which was better – beauty that the camera can't capture or beauty that is *only* really visible through a lens.

As she started to paint my lips, I focused on regaining my composure. I didn't say anything when she pressed too hard with the eyeliner and my eyes started to water, or when she pulled my hair while she was combing it out. I wanted to come across as professional, even though I knew she might have already formed a different opinion when she'd had to cover my scratches.

When she was finished, my skin had disappeared under a thick layer of make-up that was heavier than any I'd ever put on before – even when Caitlyn and I were young and we'd spent Friday nights practising putting our moms' cosmetics on each other's faces.

"So we're doing portfolio shots," Jordyn said to indicate that she was done. "Start with the dress. You can change over there."

"Over there" turned out to be another corner with a small dividing screen and very little privacy. My first outfit was a loose-fitting, low-cut dress. All of the bras I'd brought stuck out from underneath. I was trying to figure out what to do about it when Jordyn yelled to me.

"How's it going back there? We're ready to start!"

"I don't have a bra that works with this dress," I said, embarrassed and more panicky about it than I would have expected. "All the bras I brought show underneath," I explained, feeling my face and neck get hot.

Jordyn suddenly appeared from around the corner and reached around to pull the sleeves off my shoulders. "You're not supposed to wear a bra with it – it's backless, see? And it's supposed to dip low in front."

She stood back and looked at me. "You're obviously not as busty as they expected – are you sure your measurements were right? We might need to pin it up a bit." She gathered some fabric in her hands, produced a pincushion, and began manipulating the dress across my chest. She was entirely professional, like a doctor, and there was nothing indecent about the way her hands fluttered over my body. But I felt myself blushing again as she pulled the top of the dress down and over, exposing my naked breasts as she twisted and pinned the dress to hang the way they wanted it.

After what seemed like forever, she stood back and made a face. "I don't know if this one's going to work," she said. "Come with me."

She led me out into the main part of the studio where the photographer was waiting.

"Craig, what do you think about this dress?" she asked him.

"Is that all we have for formal wear?" Craig addressed Jordyn, ignoring me completely.

"Yeah – that's all they sent."

"Then we'll make it work. I'll just have to keep my eye out for those pins when I'm shooting from the front, and then we can reposition them for the back shots." Then he turned and addressed me directly for the first time. "Portfolio shots, right?" he asked. Without waiting for an answer, he continued: "This your first shoot?"

"Yes – I'm going to a convention in a couple of weeks, and Gabriella thought it would be a good idea for me to have some professional pictures," I started to explain, but he was already fiddling with reflectors and lights, obviously not concerned with the details about why I was there.

I'd seen modeling shoots on television, and Gabriella had said to just "be natural," like in the snapshots at my dad's place, so I thought I had some idea what to do. But I wanted to be sure.

"Should I just concentrate on the camera?" I asked.

"Yeah – pretend I'm not here."

I tried to do as he said and not get distracted by where I was, or why I was there. Despite what he'd said, however, concentration wasn't what Craig was actually after.

"Are you okay?" he asked, a few minutes after we'd begun.

"Why? Is something wrong?" Obviously, my question was rhetorical. Nobody stops what they're doing to ask if you are okay when everything is fine. I tensed.

"You look really serious. Could you do less serious and more sexy? And keep moving – you don't have to stand still and hold the poses. The camera can keep up."

So I tried looking "sexy." I lowered my head and raised my eyes under my heavily mascaraed lashes; I hiked my dress up a bit, being careful not to turn so much that the pins in the dress showed; I bit my lip.

"Okay – now your smile doesn't look natural – it's very forced," he sighed. "Try to relax, okay?"

I nodded, not sure what to say. I'm used to things coming very easily to me, and it was frustrating not to know how to improve my performance.

"Look at the camera," he said. "*Keep it fluid.* Pretend it belongs to one of your best friends and you're just having fun together."

I thought back and remembered a day out by Brandon's pool when he'd taken my picture and I hadn't been worried about disappointing anyone, or blowing any chances. The photos had been really nice – I liked how they'd turned out, so I took some deep breaths and decided that these photos, like those we'd taken at Brandon's house, would also be *for me.*

Craig noticed the change as soon as I worked it out in my mind.

"Okay, good. *Relax. Just like that.* Trust yourself."

Realizing that I already knew how to do what he was asking made all the difference.

Craig stopped directing me and *I* almost stopped worrying about disappointing everyone. I changed outfits a couple of times – first into a sweater and pants that were supposed to be for serious shots, and then into casual clothes, with my hair pulled up in a high ponytail for some "sporty" shots.

Just as I was actually starting to feel like "Sporty Ashley," we were done.

"Okay. I'll have the proofs to Gabriella in a couple of days," Craig said as he began walking around turning off the lights.

"So, that's it?" I wasn't sure whether there was something else I should be doing.

"That's it," he said, and I took it as my cue to change and get out.

I caught another glimpse of myself in the mirror as I picked up my bag. "Can I wash this make-up off before I leave?" I asked Jordyn. She looked surprised, but she nodded and pointed me toward a sink as she asked, "You don't like it?" She sounded hurt.

"It just … feels a little heavy for such a hot day," I said truthfully.

It turned out that the really heavy part of my day was still to come.

When I arrived back at my mom's place, I discovered a letter from Brandon.

*June 27*

*Dear Ashley,*
*How are you? I hope you are okay and that everything is good*

at the shelter. Did you get homes for all those kittens yet?

Camp is fine, so far, and I love being out in the canoes, but it's hard work because we're up early in the morning and the kids in my cabin don't like to go to sleep too early. I miss you and I think about you all the time. One of the other counsellors is named Ashley, and every time someone calls her or talks about her, I turn around expecting to see you.

Not talking to you is a lot harder than I thought it would be, and it feels weird to tell people here that I am single when they ask.

Do you remember the light-up turtle pendant you got me out of the vending machine last year? I brought it with me (as a joke but also because it reminded me of you) and everyone loves it. The kids all want to borrow it when they go out to the bathroom after dark, because they can pretend they are cool – and they don't have to use a flashlight.

Write me back when you can.
Sincerely,
Brandon

Reading it, I felt sad and mad again, all at the same time. "Not talking to you is a lot harder than I thought it would be"? Well, duh! How could he not have thought it would be difficult after being together for two years? But then again, I also wouldn't have thought that after two years he would choose a cheap plastic turtle necklace as a reminder of me. What had happened to the compass watch I'd given him at Christmas?

And "it feels weird to tell people I'm single"? The only people I'd talked to about it were Caitlyn and my parents.

Who exactly was *he* telling? And wasn't "being single" what he'd wanted?

And then, there were his closing words: *Sincerely*. Not "love," not "Your friend always," just "sincerely." "Ex-girlfriend Ashley." Ouch.

Even though I was hurt, I wanted to be mature and friendly, out of respect for all the things we'd shared over the years. I tried to write back to him.

*June 30th*

*Dear Brandon,*

*It was nice to hear from you. I am fine, and I actually have some very big news. Last week my dad introduced me to his new girlfriend (I know, I was shocked too!!!) and she runs a modeling school. She said she thinks I have an excellent chance to make it as a professional model, so I had some portfolio shots taken today.*

I re-read what I'd written and ripped it up. It couldn't have sounded more fake if I'd tried – "I'm fine and I'm going to try to be a professional model"? True or not, it was either going to sound as if I was bragging or like a pathetic attempt to win back his attention, neither of which I wanted.

I knew he was trying to be nice, trying to sweeten me up by writing to me, but it was clear that I couldn't be pen pals with him yet. I still couldn't lie in bed and picture him with another girl without getting tense and feeling sick all over again, like that the night on the hill.

My mom – a true break-up expert – sympathized with

me about Brandon's letter after dinner.

"He misses you, Ash – just like you miss him," she said. "But you're right, it's probably still too raw and fresh for you to write back to him now, even though you do have wonderful news to share. Don't worry. Someday, the wound *will* heal. It'll be like my cancer – it'll make you stronger. The scar will be there, but the pain will be gone."

As much as I was missing Brandon, Mom's comparison of The Break-Up to her cancer kind of put things in perspective. I wasn't ready to share my modeling news with him, but I *was* ready to see the photos I hoped would make everyone proud of me and channel my Brandon-frustration into modeling success.

# CHAPTER 10

Three days later, I had dinner at Caitlyn's and arrived back at my dad's to find him, Gabriella, *and my mother* out in the backyard, going over my portfolio pictures.

"Hi, Mom. What are you doing here?" I asked. She hardly ever comes to my dad's – partly because she's allergic to Daphne, but also, I suspected, because she and Dad weren't a couple anymore and I was the only thing they really still had in common.

She glanced quickly at my dad, then back at me. "Well, your father and I thought it made sense for me to meet Gabriella since she's going to be taking you to the convention in a few weeks. So when he said she was bringing the proofs over, I thought it would be a good opportunity for us all to chat. Besides, I couldn't wait to see your pictures!"

Gabriella looked totally poised and cool – even though the night was super-muggy. She was wearing a pale pink sundress that laced up the back. Mom looked equally sophisticated in a sleeveless white blouse and capri pants. Once again, I felt scruffy in my tank top and shorts, but it was the most practical thing to wear for dog-walking and kennel cleaning. I'm sure that my mom was horrified to see me that way, and I was a bit embarrassed, too, with Gabriella there – but *she* didn't seem to mind.

As always, Gabriella got right to the point. "I have your portfolio right here. We aren't starting with a lot," she explained, "obviously due to the time factor, but the shots are excellent. I knew I was right about you – you're definitely going to get some contract offers at the convention."

Then she handed me a 5x7 photo album with a glossy close-up of a smiling face on the cover.

"This is totally surreal," I puzzled. "I *know* it's me, but it doesn't *look* like me … I've never seen myself look anything remotely like this … in *any* photo."

"That's the magic of a good team, right there," she said. "A gorgeous girl, skilful make-up, a great photographer … and you get something really special." She encouraged me to flip through the rest of the book, and I saw that she'd chosen two close-ups, a profile, a three-quarter length shot, and a full-length picture to emphasize my full height.

Mom and Dad were murmuring something on the far side of the patio, but I didn't catch it because I was still trying to figure out what it was about the pictures that was throwing me off so much. The photos were *obviously* me, but I appeared different – older, more mature. It fascinated me how the make-up that had been so thick and dark in the mirror was subtle and almost unnoticeable in most of the pictures, except for the last ones, where Jordyn had deepened the eye and lip color for variety. In all of them, my eyes gleamed. I had the sense of wanting to know more about the girl in the photo, even though I was looking at pictures of myself.

"Did they touch these up digitally or anything?" I asked, still in shock over how different I looked in them.

"No, digital adjustments are made all the time in print work, but portfolio shots should always be unaltered," she explained. "I have the two headshots blown-up in here," she said, handing me a large brown envelope. "You'll need those for the convention. Your application to attend was approved by the board and your parents have signed the permissions, so I'll get your registration in tomorrow."

"Do you *really* think we can make this happen?" I asked directly. By this time, there was no question that I wanted it – a modeling career. However, if there was any chance that she was being overly optimistic because of my dad, I needed to know – *before* I set myself up for possible failure and public humiliation. I watched her face carefully while she answered.

Smiling sincerely, she said, "We *can* make it happen, Ashley – we already are." Then, her face sharpened, and she added, "And I know it's hard for you, because you are *so* bright and *so* independent, but you have to *trust* me and my experience. Can you do that?"

The fact that she called me "bright" and "independent" probably caused me to trust her even more than I already did. I knew she was subtly hinting at the scratches on my arms, and I appreciated her being delicate about it, especially in front of my mom.

"I can do it," I said with certainty as my parents

wandered back toward us.

"Excellent." She smiled warmly again and directed her next comment to my mom. "All the rules and regulations are in this envelope, and I've pre-booked Ashley's hotel room." She turned back toward me. "I've got you sharing with another one of my girls – you're the same age, and she's got some experience that I think you'll find helpful."

As much as I appreciated Gabriella's coaching, and everything she was doing for me, I was grateful that she'd had the foresight to put me with someone who'd already done some modeling, but who was my own age. I hoped we could be friends.

"You're going to be there, too, though, right?" I asked her.

"Yes," she said as she glanced back at my mother, "but I'm judging in the children's division and conducting some seminars for other modeling schools, so I'll be busy. You won't see me in a competitive setting.

"Now," she continued, "you will notice in that literature that part of the convention includes a runway competition. Obviously at 5'9" we're more interested in print work for you, because many agencies prefer their girls taller on the catwalk, but you could still have occasional runway opportunities, so entering will be good practice. Since you've never taken any classes in runway walking and we're so short on time, I was hoping we could go over a few of the basics tomorrow at my office. Then you can practice over the next couple of weeks. Okay?"

Other people – *normal people* – would have thought that was a fantastic idea, but me being "Type-A Ashley," I couldn't wait that long. I knew that I needed to go into the convention as prepared as possible and I was anxious because I didn't feel as if two weeks was enough time. I *hated* having to ask for help – she'd been right when she'd called me "independent" – but more than that, I hated feeling unprepared. I had to ask.

"Tomorrow would be okay," I said, hoping she understood that I really was committed to trusting her judgment, "but is there any chance you could give me a primer right now? I could still come in tomorrow, but it would give me something to work on tonight."

"Ashley." My mom, who had been uncharacteristically silent throughout the exchange, now looked at me pointedly. "Gabriella is here to visit your father, and she's already used up enough time explaining everything to me. She might just want to relax."

Gabriella laughed and shook her head. "I don't know the meaning of the word!" She gestured for me to follow her inside.

"See, Mom?" I whispered on my way by her. "She's just like us."

"And you think that's a good thing?" my mom joked back. "Your father won't be able to put up with three of us!" It was cool that my mom was able to joke about Dad's new girlfriend. It gave me hope that someday I'd get to the point where I could do that with Brandon.

By the time I'd said goodnight to my mom and had gone

inside, Gabriella had already pulled all of my dad's dining room chairs over to one side of the room so that there was a long, clear space running straight through the length of the house, from the living room in front, through the attached dining room, and into the kitchen.

"This is your runway," she gestured. "*Yours*. Walk like it's there for you and nobody else. For now, we just want to get you comfortable out there. Eventually, though, you'll want to develop a signature walk – something that says "there's Ashley. Like this." She stood still for a minute, posing with her right hand on her hip, then she started walking with her chin up, and a long, controlled stride. Gabriella walked like someone who knows where she's going and isn't going to stop until she gets there. Her body language said, "You're welcome to come along, but don't try to hold me back." *I* wanted to be that person. I'd spent my whole life trying to be that person. I wanted to walk like that person. I stepped forward confidently and followed her.

"That's excellent," she encouraged me after she'd watched me do a few lengths of our improvised catwalk. "Most girls don't have that kind of confidence when they first start, but you've already got it."

In truth, as I walked, I was thinking about the way I hoped I had looked as I walked away from Brandon that night on the hill, when I'd felt so broken inside but hadn't wanted him to see it.

# CHAPTER 11

I worked with Gabriella for half an hour, and then, after dark, I practiced on the sidewalk while I took Daphne out for her evening walk. It was easy with her because she's so well trained, she can read my movements and easily keep up with me no matter what I do.

The next day, at the animal shelter, I tried to practice some more while I walked the dogs there. Rescued dogs *are* very trainable, but they've usually lived with people who didn't actually have the time or the knowledge to train them. So they often came to us not knowing the basics, like how to walk on a leash without pulling. Making them try to keep up with my "Ashley-with-Attitude-Signature-Stride" seemed like it would be perfect practice for all of us, since the best way to train them is to just keep walking, no matter what they do. It sounds mean, if you don't understand it, but teaching them to stay close to you on a leash is really about keeping them safe from passing cars and other hazards. Sadly for me, when I tried my runway walk with the bigger dogs, it turned out that none of us was as ready as I'd hoped. In a pathetic flashback to my shoelace stubbornness as a child, I landed painfully on my butt several times.

When I began trying on bathing suits at the mall with Caitlyn later that afternoon, I realized I had a couple of big red blotches from my falls that would darken into real bruises later on. We were hunting for something I could wear in the swimsuit competition at the convention. Everyone knows that finding a bathing suit that's comfortable *and* flattering is always a challenge, but it felt especially daunting when I knew I was going to be *formally* judged on my appearance in it. I knew a second opinion would really help. Plus, spending more time with Caitlyn since Brandon had left was making me realize how much I'd missed our "girl time." So when she'd volunteered to come along, I was doubly happy.

My first pick was a chic blue one-piece suit. It was very different from anything I normally would have chosen because it had green and turquoise sequinned trim around the low neck-line and high-cut legs. "What happened to you?" Caitlyn asked with wide eyes as I emerged from the dressing room with it on.

At first, I thought she was talking about the sequins, which I'd expected to look kind of mermaid-y, but actually seemed more "Las Vegas lounge lizard" once I had the bathing suit on. Then I saw that Caitlyn was pointing to the monster bruise that was developing on my left hip.

"Let's just say it was some multi-tasking gone very, very wrong," I said. "How's the suit look?"

"Okay, so no multi-tasking right now," she said, still grimacing from the sight of my bruise. "Singular focus. For sure *not* that one," she said, curling her lip, wrinkling her nose, and shaking her head at the blue suit. "Have you decided for sure against getting a bikini?" she asked, holding up a few pieces of string that were apparently supposed to count as a bathing suit.

"I don't know yet, but definitely *not* that!" I said. "No thongs allowed."

"But it would have looked so good on you!" she teased, waving it in the air before handing me a few others to try. "Try these, then."

I spent the next hour popping in and out of the change room like a bird in a cuckoo clock, while Caitlyn and a salesgirl brought me suit after suit. I tried on sporty suits, sexy suits, string bikinis (no thong!), and tankinis with boy-shorts.

"They all look fantastic on you," Caitlyn said after we'd narrowed it down to three or four, "but with your long torso and lean abs, I think you should go with the red one. It shows off what you have, but it still kind of keeps it together, if you know what I mean."

"The red one" was technically a one-piece suit, but it had cut-outs across the back and stomach areas, so the top and bottom of the suit were joined by thin strips of fabric at the sides, making it look a lot like a bikini when it was on.

"It's not really *me* though," I protested, picturing myself showing my dad, who had agreed – surprisingly – to continue paying for all of my modeling-related expenses. "I've never considered myself the 'sexy' type."

"But you *could* be sexy if you wanted," Caitlyn said. "So

get the red one."

I didn't want to look as if I was trying too hard. "How about the purple tankini?" I asked again.

Caitlyn shook her head and stood firm. Ever since she'd broken up with Tyler, she'd been much more sure of herself than ever before, and she didn't look like she was going to back down. "Modeling isn't about *you*," she said. "It's about selling someone an *idea* of who you are and making them think they can be that, too. You need to get the red one."

She was sure, but I was undecided, which wasn't at all like me. I prefer to just make the best decisions I can with the best information I have, rather than dragging stuff out – hence, the scene on the hill with Brandon. I was still struggling to choose a suit, though, when I looked up and saw Brandon's mom enter the store.

She'd already spotted us and was heading our way before I could duck back into the change room.

"Ashley! Caitlyn! What a nice surprise to see you both! I've missed you this summer."

"H-hi," was all I could get out before she started talking again.

"You've had your hair done! It's beautiful. Have you heard from Brandon? He's only written to us once so far, and I told his father he must be saving all his strength for writing to you … I know letters seem so old-fashioned to you kids. He was thinking it would be a real challenge to go away for an entire summer without email and text messaging …"

I held onto the door of the changing room and took a

deep breath. "He wrote to me once, last week," I told her.

"Only once?"

"Yes, I – "

"Oh, I'm sure he really misses you – they just keep them so busy at camp. I see that you girls are buying new swimsuits! Why don't you come over one afternoon and use the pool?"

"Ashley's doing some modeling this summer and she needs a new suit for a competition," Caitlyn told her. I was sure *I* wouldn't have had the courage to mention it to Brandon's mom, but I was kind of relieved that Caitlyn had. It still felt weird that Brandon, who'd shared so much with me, didn't know about this big thing going on in my life right now. And this way, he'd hear for sure.

"Modeling? Ashley – that's wonderful! Brandon didn't mention anything about it in his letter ... does he know?"

"No, I – it came up very suddenly ..." I stammered.

"Well, come on over for a swim one day and tell me all about it. Brandon will be so proud to tell everyone his girlfriend's a model!"

She leaned in and gave me a kiss on the cheek and a hug.

And that's when I realized that not only was she completely unaware that we'd broken up, but she'd had nothing – absolutely nothing – to do with it.

# CHAPTER 12

Brandon's mom was still talking, and I was starting to feel faint. Caitlyn covered for me.

"That burger's really not sitting well, is it, Ash? You're looking a little white." She turned back to Brandon's mom. "It was so nice to see you …"

"Right – take care, girls, and please remember the pool is always available to you."

"She doesn't know, does she?" I asked Caitlyn after Brandon's mom left.

"Not a clue. Ash, I never thought I'd say this, but I think Brandon lied to you. He just used his mom as an excuse."

I'd never felt like such a loser – I was determined not to be one. Just because I had never felt more undesirable in my entire life didn't mean I had to *look* it.

"I'm getting the *red* suit," I said.

\* \* \*

Later, at the food court, I tried to avoid all mention of my former boyfriend's betrayal and focus the conversation on modeling.

"Okay – now I'm thinking that maybe Brandon's mom is just embarrassed that she caused the break-up, so she's pretending she didn't know," Caitlyn said over a plate of fries. "And why aren't you eating? Don't tell me you're giving up french fries on me now that you're a model."

Glad she had made a joke, but still in shock, I gave her a half-smile. Normally, I *would* have shared the fries with her, but seeing Brandon's mom had made me lose my appetite completely.

"She didn't know," I whispered with certainty, forcing back the tears that were fighting their way up. "She didn't have anything to do with it, even though he told me it was because of his mom." Obviously, he'd just used his mom as an excuse to break up with me, and if it didn't have anything to do with *her*, then it was all about *me*. I was too humiliated to talk about it, even to my best friend.

I took another deep breath and faked a smile. "Let's talk about modeling, okay?"

She nodded. "Okay, fashion-talk it is ... What are you going to wear for the runway competition?"

"I don't have a lot of choices – it says I have to wear black, white, or a combination of black and white ... which either means we buy something today, or I'm heading down the runway in a T-shirt and shorts – which would mortify my mother." I was trying to channel my hurt feelings into action.

"I think you could pull off the T-shirt and shorts if you *had* to," Caitlyn said, "but in runway modeling you're moving down the catwalk to show off the clothes as if they were part of you. So maybe you should wear something that moves. Something fun."

"Okay," I said, feeling bolder and better already because I had a plan of action back underway. "I'm also wondering if I should be trying out some different make-up looks … with more color."

Caitlyn knows when to push me to take more risks – like with the red swimsuit – and when to rein me back in. That's why we're a good team. Once again, she didn't let me down. "I don't think this is the time to start experimenting with different make-up, especially now that you have new hair," she said. "But from a practical point of view, you might want to make sure all your make-up brushes are super clean so that you aren't smudging colors around on your face when you're applying blush. Don't start messing with something that's already working, though. Remember when all those girls had their hair done up for yearbook photos, and then they all cried because the pictures didn't look like them?"

She was right, but secretly, I wished different hair and make-up *could* turn me into someone else – someone like the confident girl I used to think I was – with the hot boyfriend and all.

We spent the rest of the afternoon shopping, and Caitlyn chose a sleeveless black chiffon dress for me. It had an empire waist and a flowing skirt.

"Do you think it's current enough for the fashion world?" I asked.

"It's classic, almost like something vintage," she reassured me, sensing the self-doubt behind my question.

"I just want it to be okay…" I said.

"It *will* be okay," she told me, giving me a hug. "It's perfect, whether you recognize it or not."

I took the hint and tried to focus on everything that was going well. Luckily, having the swimsuit and the dress picked out made it easier for me to concentrate on everything else I had to do before my trip. I tried on my new swimsuit for Gabriella later that afternoon at my dad's. She agreed that I'd made a good choice, but then she spotted my bruises, which had turned black and purple by the time she saw them. Her forehead creased and she worked her jaw back and forth a little bit before she spoke. By this time, she knew me well enough not to even ask where the bruises had come from.

"Listen, Ashley," she said. "I know you *love* working with those animals – and it's great, it really is. But right now, you have to think about your appearance and make sure you look your absolute best at the convention. You had scratches all over your hands the other day, and now you're covered in *bruises*! Is there any way you could take some time off from the shelter? Just until the convention? It could be a little rest, to renew your body and mind. You're just a volunteer there – I'm sure they'd understand."

The shelter *would* understand, but I was starting to see that *Gabriella* didn't really understand why I loved being there. Now I had to figure out a way to thrive in two very different worlds.

# CHAPTER 13

During dinner that night at my dad's place, Gabriella brought up the issue – again – of me taking some time off from the shelter. I was used to my mom and dad having different perspectives on things, but I usually only had to deal with one of them at a time. So, as much as my dad's infatuation with Gabriella was cute, it was frustrating to have to support my position to two adults simultaneously. My dad sided with Gabriella, approaching it from the perspective of not wanting to waste all the money he'd put into my portfolio and clothing already.

I didn't fault Gabriella for asking me to give up something I loved, because she wasn't an animal person. It was obvious in the way she patted Daphne – on the head, with a fully extended arm and an open palm – that she wasn't a genuine dog person. *Real* dog lovers, like me, hug them and nuzzle them and rub their bellies without even thinking twice about it. We can't help ourselves.

*She* couldn't really understand how hard it would be, but I would have expected my dad, who'd never really been into fashion, to support my volunteer work a little more. I suspected that maybe he was having his own issues of "divided loyalty" between me and Gabriella.

Not wanting to completely give up on the shelter, I negotiated a compromise with them. I spent my time just cleaning the litter and the pens, without really walking or playing with any of the animals. It wasn't perfect, but it was better than not going at all. And it kept all the adults happy.

Poor little Raven – the black cat I'd told Brandon about – was still at the shelter. Her kittens had all been adopted, but she wouldn't be adoptable until her milk dried up and she could be spayed. For her, I cheated just a little and petted her every day, because she was so gentle, and I knew she'd be there for a while. If she never did anything fun, eventually she'd go crazy and she wouldn't be adoptable at all.

As much as *she* needed to get away from the shelter, I felt like I needed to be there. Even when I was helping out with paperwork in the office, being at the shelter helped distract me from obsessing about the upcoming convention, and all the ways I was or wasn't ready.

During the next two weeks, Gabriella said my walk was becoming very natural. I practiced whenever I could, but I was still wishing I'd had time to take classes. In desperation, I'd been watching even more fashion programs on TV, trying to identify the models who had "signature strides" and figure out what made them special. Like Gabriella, most of them seemed to strut very deliberately, moving their hips around and leaning slightly backward. There was one in particular that I'd been trying to copy, because she was the one who seemed to be the best. Even when she had to wear really ugly clothes – and a lot of the models did – she walked as if she was proud of them. That made the clothes seem a lot more desirable.

Confidence can make everything seem better than it is. For example, everyone's always debating why girls love "bad boys," but actually, I think it's very simple. "Bad boys" are confident. Confidence is appealing. Therefore, "bad boys" are appealing. It doesn't mean they're *good* for you – or that the ugly clothes on a confident model will look good on you – but it's the confidence that makes you want them.

Gabriella's confidence made *me* want to be like *her*.

When I thought I was starting to get good at the whole walking thing, I had Caitlyn make a videotape of me doing my walk in a whole bunch of different outfits, including the dress I'd bought for the convention. Watching it with her was hard. Even though Caitlyn had been there and had *seen* all my mistakes, I worried that she'd think I was wasting her time – I'd been practicing all week, and it still wasn't perfect. Together, we picked out all the things that I did awkwardly or stiffly or too quickly or too slowly, so I could work on correcting those faults. I tried strutting and looking bored, like the professionals, while Caitlyn videotaped me again. "I hate to tell you this," she'd said, as we watched the first couple of takes, "but you look kind of constipated!"

"That's because I'm so uptight about this," I admitted. "I'm sorry we have to keep going over the same things."

"So just relax already – you can do this," she said.

"You know I can't relax!" I said. "I can't even fool a

*computer* into thinking I'm relaxed."

She looked at me as if maybe I'd finally gone crazy, so I explained. "This morning at the shelter, everyone was doing this online quiz called: 'If You Were a Dog, What Kind Would You Be?' and you had to answer a bunch of questions about totally unrelated things so that it could assess your personality. All the other people who did the quiz got pegged as fun, happy-go-lucky breeds, like Labs. But you know what it said I am?"

"I don't know – a Golden Retriever, like Daphne?" she guessed.

"No – a Border Collie," I said, pulling out the page I'd printed and reading from it. "'Border Collies are intelligent, and they have a strong work ethic, but they also have a tendency toward obsession or compulsions.'" Reading it again made me want to re-take the test and get a different breed, which was just obsessive enough to make me realize how accurate it actually was.

"How does a dog get obsessed?" Caitlyn asked.

"They just go overboard on the details, the same as me," I explained. "Like, when they're *supposed* to be herding sheep and watching for predators, sometimes they stress too much about the whole thing and they end up chasing bugs, shadows, or anything else that moves. It's all here."

"That's you all right," she nodded.

I pretended to hit her with the paper. "It's not funny!" Even Caitlyn didn't really know the true depths of my own "detail overload." I hadn't admitted it to her, because it seemed kind of pathetic, but despite all the things I had to do before the convention, I was still worrying about irrelevant stuff like whether or not Brandon's mom had told him about seeing me at the mall.

"You know what's most pathetic about their compulsions?" I asked, before answering my own question. "They've been *bred* that way – for hundreds of years – it's just in them, and they can't help it."

"So?"

"So, look at my mother! Always worrying about where stuff goes and what everyone around her is doing and whether or not her cancer treatments are going to make her late for work. Obviously, it's been bred into *me*! Add to that the fact than I'm an only child *and* the product of a failed marriage, and I can't help but be messed up!" I was only half-serious, but it still felt better to talk about it out loud.

"Don't blame your parents for this one!" she teased. "*You're* the one walking like you need to go to the bathroom!" And even though I knew she wasn't at all serious, I also knew she was right; I needed to keep practicing because I was the only one who could make it better, and I did not want to let anyone down.

Several tries later, I was finally starting to see some progress.

Caitlyn also helped me work out a thirty-second script for the television-acting competition. Although I was allowed to use a published script, I wanted to do something original so the judges couldn't compare my delivery to that of other competitors. Judging was going to be based on "projection, pronunciation, humor, and believability."

I'd thought about doing a mock ad for the animal shelter, or for having your pets spayed and neutered. I figured I'd have more believability if I talked about something I truly cared about. Gabriella didn't think it was a good idea to go that route, however, because she said that it could be too political for the judges. Obviously, I knew she was the expert, but it bugged me that I couldn't talk about my passions, so I still kind of wanted to do it my way.

"Wouldn't I be more convincing if I cared about the subject matter?" I asked Mom later that week, still sure I was right and hoping to sway her to my side.

"Convincing? Or *successful*?" she asked. "Because I'm sure you can talk about anything you like up there – but I've told you so many times, Ashley – if you want to be *successful*, sometimes you have to do what's expected of you, instead of what you want." Which, loosely translated, meant "I expect you to do what Gabriella recommends, because I expect you to be successful." Ultimately, I came up with a fictional commercial for a sleepwear store called "The Cat's Pyjamas."

Caitlyn helped me rehearse my script in front of the camera, too.

Finally, in addition to practicing my walk and my commercial, I started making lists. The biggest one had three columns: stuff I still needed to buy, stuff to pack, and stuff to do before I left.

Even though years of moving between my parents'

houses had turned me into a seasoned packer, I found it difficult to narrow down what I needed to bring with me. I decided it was better to bring too many things than not enough, because I didn't want to get there, wish I'd brought something I'd ruled out, and then spend the whole time regretting it.

I began my packing with the clothes that were at my mom's house – clean, dry, and ready to go. After that I did laundry to retrieve other things I'd need, and I created a sub-list of things I had to look for at my dad's. Listing and packing and organizing kept me focused on things that I could control, like my appearance, rather than things I couldn't, like my competition.

Gabriella looked over my things with me just before the convention.

"It looks excellent, Ashley," she said. "What you need to do now is just rest – get a good night's sleep because it's going to be a *very* busy weekend."

I know most people like to relax whenever possible, but *I* was relieved to hear that the weekend was going to be busy.

If I'd known what the convention really had in store for me, I wouldn't have been able to sleep at all.

# CHAPTER 14

The drama began subtly before I even left home.

Gabriella had offered to drive me to the convention, and as with the photo shoot, my mom seemed kind of disappointed in being left out. Although I suspected that part of her was relieved to be able to carry on with her normal routines and not have to take off work Friday afternoon for me, her frustration came through in a few bitter comments about the lack of formal chaperoning at the event, and about how Gabriella "better be a good driver."

When Gabriella arrived to get me, my next challenge ended up being the lack of trunk space in her bright yellow Jeep. The Jeep only had two seats up front with a small cargo area in behind, and we struggled to fit my bags beside her things in the tiny space. Instead of regretting not bringing *enough*, I was already regretting having brought so much. After a few minutes of rearranging, we managed to squish everything in and get on our way.

The GPS said it was going to take us two hours and seventeen minutes to get to the other side of the city for the convention. I didn't want to drive Gabriella crazy with any more questions about what to expect, so I decided it might finally be a good time to get to know her as my dad's girlfriend – apart from her role as my modeling mentor.

"So, how did you meet my dad anyway?" I asked as we pulled onto the freeway.

"Oh – didn't he tell you?" she laughed. "I was volunteering at the hospital, with the beauty program for cancer patients called 'Looking good, Looking up' and your dad had brought your mom for one of her oncology appointments. I ended up in an elevator with him and I saw a five dollar bill on the floor – I quickly picked it up and told him he must have dropped it. He didn't think it was his, but we started talking. And then we ended up spending the money to go for coffee together in the cafeteria."

"No, actually, he didn't tell me anything about that," I said, thinking less about the story than about why neither one of my parents had told me that my dad was attending doctors' appointments with my mom. I hadn't even realized that Gabriella knew my mom had been sick.

"Well, once we started talking, and he explained that he was there with his ex-wife, I just thought to myself, 'What an amazing man! He's supportive of his ex, and he obviously doesn't have any hang-ups about his prior relationships ... I have to get to know him better.' So I asked him out."

"Wow!" I thought it was pretty cool that *Gabriella* had done the asking out. I also realized again that I could take a hint from my parents and quit worrying about whether or not Brandon had met anyone else yet. No matter what his reasons had been for breaking up with me, he *had* cared about me once. I suddenly felt very certain that he would still go anywhere for me that I needed him to, just as my dad was obviously still supportive of my mom.

"And how did you get involved with that beauty program?" I asked when I was ready to talk again.

"Well," she said slowly as if she couldn't quite remember, "I guess it kind of happened in the same way that you got involved with the shelter. I was already passionate about the beauty industry, the way you're passionate about animals. I'd been modeling professionally for several years, and then I got sick and I ended up coming back here, to stay with my parents until I was healthy again."

"How long did that take?" I asked, not knowing what she'd been sick with, but feeling that it would be rude to ask directly.

"Eight months – at some point during my travels, I had contracted a form of hepatitis," she said. "I'm fine now, but getting better was a long, slow process. Toward the end of my recovery, I was at the hospital for a check-up, and I started talking to a couple of women who were there for cancer treatments. They confessed to me that the change in their physical appearance was one of the hardest things – psychologically – about being sick. Even if you don't lose your hair through chemotherapy, cancer treatments can cause all kinds of physical changes, like dry, discolored skin and dark circles under the eyes."

"I guess if you don't recognize the face in the mirror, it *is* kind of hard to feel like yourself," I said, remembering how odd it had felt seeing my portfolio shots – and *they* were a *big* improvement over my usual appearance. Having to be sick *and* look different would be a lot to take.

"So by the time I was healthy again," she continued, "I'd kind of lost my edge, and the modeling jobs just weren't coming in like they had before. I'd done a lot of thinking while I was sick, though, and I realized that there were still a lot of things I wanted to do with my life, and that I couldn't keep waiting for 'someday.' That's when I opened the modeling school, started the beauty program at the hospital, and vowed to only work six months every year."

"But, wasn't it hard to give up on modeling?"

She turned to me quickly, and I could see that she was emotional but was trying to keep her voice upbeat. "It was. I'm very happy with my life, and I'm involved in the industry in different ways now. But there's really no world like modeling. You'll see what I mean."

My first real glimpse of that world came shortly after our arrival at the hotel.

I knew there'd be some beautiful girls at the modeling convention, but I guess I'd been thinking a lot about what Jordyn, the make-up artist, had said, and I'd convinced myself that most of the people there were probably just regular-looking before they had their hair and make-up done. That is, until I opened the door to my hotel room and met my roommate.

*She* was the first person I had ever met who passed "the baldness test." It was Caitlyn who'd told me about it. Because she's an artist, she breaks things down visually to their most basic forms, and she taught me that one of the things the human eye finds beautiful in study after study is symmetry – and you can often get a better idea of how symmetrical someone's face is by imagining how she'd look without her hair.

Hair makes a bigger difference than people might think. Sometimes, someone will strike you as really stunning – but if you imagine her hair away, you'll often see that really her hair is her best feature, or that one side of her mouth is just slightly higher than the other – like mine – or something like that. I find it kind of reassuring, because it reminds me that *everyone's* imperfect in some way, but that there's almost always a way to compensate.

I didn't even have to imagine Shayla bald, because when I arrived, she'd just taken a shower and her hair was wrapped up in a towel when she opened the door.

She had perfect, flawless skin, with no freckles, no blemishes, and no discolorations at all. Her turquoise eyes were so bright, and so perfectly almond shaped, that they drew your attention right to them. All of her features seemed perfectly symmetrical, too. I caught my breath in a mixture of surprise and envy, realizing that this was a girl who didn't even need hair.

"Are you Ashley?" she asked.

When I nodded, she smiled and introduced herself. "I'm Shayla. It's nice to meet you! Sorry I made such a mess with my stuff already," she said, leading me into the room we'd be sharing, which was already littered with clothing and accessories. With just a quick glance, I counted more than six pairs of shoes and boots. I saw a lot of black and white, so I guessed that either she hadn't had any problem finding runway clothes, or she still hadn't decided what she'd be wearing.

"I'll hang the clothes up later," she offered, as she hauled a bunch of her stuff off one bed and dropped it on the other.

"No problem," I said, thinking, for once in my life, that even getting stuff organized wasn't going to ease the jitters I was feeling, and wondering again how I'd gotten into this whole thing – where I might fail *publicly* – in the first place. Still, out of habit, I hung my garment bag in the closet as I entered the room and placed my suitcase carefully on the rack beside the empty bed.

"I don't mean to be rude, but I have to go dry my hair before it gets too frizzy," Shayla said, heading into the bathroom before we'd had a chance to talk about anything else.

"Okay," I called after her, a bit disappointed that I couldn't get to know her yet, but not hating the idea of having a few moments alone to unpack and to read some of the stuff they'd given me downstairs at registration.

As I heard the hair dryer start, I turned my attention to the first piece of paper they'd given me – the one marked "National Modeling Association Modeling Convention RULES AND REGULATIONS." It was the same list Gabriella had given me two weeks before, so I'd practically memorized it already.

There were almost two pages of rules, which would have driven Caitlyn crazy, but they actually made me feel secure, because I knew exactly what was – and what wasn't – permitted. "All contestants must follow these rules and regulations or they will be subject to disqualification. Contestants are NOT allowed to speak personally to the agents." That one had worried me at first. But Gabriella explained that she wasn't there as an agent looking for new talent – she was there as someone *bringing* models. So it was okay to talk to her if I saw her. Still, we'd agreed that it might be best if we kept her relationship with my dad quiet, because she didn't want anyone to think she played favorites. And *I* didn't want anyone – myself included – to think I couldn't be successful doing this all on my own.

I hadn't had the nerve to ask Gabriella whether the judges had their own versions of "the baldness test" and whether or not I'd pass.

The convention was a chance for smaller, local agencies like Gabriella's to have their students evaluated by agents from some of the world's top modeling agencies, such as I*deal* and *Elegance* in New York, *Belles Filles* in Paris, as well as agencies in London and Milan. When I'd finished reading everything, I picked up my cell and gave my mom a quick call to let her know I'd arrived.

Her office line rang several times before going right into an outgoing message indicating that she was unavailable for the afternoon, but to please leave a message. I couldn't remember the last time she'd taken an afternoon off, and she hadn't mentioned anything about it earlier, so I tried her cell. She picked up on the third ring.

"Hello, darling! Did you make it okay?"

"Yeah, that's what I was calling to tell you ... where are you? Your voicemail said you were out of the office."

She didn't hesitate at all which made me feel silly as she explained, "Oh, I'm just not in *my* office this afternoon. I guess I should have made it clearer on my voicemail."

"Oh, all right." I still didn't really understand what she was talking about, but I wasn't in the mood for a long conversation. "That reminds me, I can't take my phone down to the events with me, so please don't panic if you can't reach me."

"I won't. Have some fun, okay?"

"I'll try," I told her, wanting to have fun, but knowing my need to do well would probably make it hard to lighten up.

"Ashley? Do your best. This is a once in a lifetime opportunity and you really need to grab it."

"I will."

"And remember, Gabriella said she'd keep an eye out for you, which is the only reason you don't have *me* there chaperoning you ... so don't choose this weekend to do anything crazy okay?"

"I know. Bye, Mom." I rolled my eyes, wondering if it would have been better not to have called her at all. I mean, seriously – I'd been with my boyfriend for *two years*, and I hadn't slept with him – how "crazy" did she think I was going to get in one random weekend?

I was just hanging up as Shayla came out of the bathroom with her hair dried and styled long and smooth.

"Mother checking up on you?" she asked with a giggle.

"Kind of ... my dad's girlfriend offered to drive me here and back, and even though my mom's trying to be cool about it, I think she wishes it had been her." I figured if I didn't say "my dad's girlfriend, who happens to be Gabriella McCullough," I wasn't really giving away any big secrets.

"Oh. How long have your parents been split?" she asked.

"They've been divorced for years," I explained, "and I don't think Mom's actually even jealous of the woman being with my dad, but my mom seems a little bit annoyed about her spending the time with me, even though I needed the rides."

"I'm so glad I don't have to deal with crap like that anymore," Shayla said rolling her eyes. "I got a car last month, and it's unbelievable how much freedom it buys you – you should get one."

"Having a car would be totally superior to taking my bike everywhere," I said. "But my mom's a stress-case, and my dad's *usually* a bit of a cheapskate so there's no way they'd get me my own car right now – that's one thing they'd totally agree on." I didn't actually mind using my bike for transportation, but I didn't want to sound unimpressed by the fact that she had her own car.

She tilted her head to one side and stuck her bottom lip out in mock pity for me, before suddenly becoming animated again and telling me, "Actually, I bought mine myself. With money I made doing catalogues last year."

"Really? You made enough to buy a car?"

"It's used, but yeah – I pay my own insurance, too."

"Well, like I said, my mom's a huge worrier, but she's

just finished breast cancer treatments, so I think me getting a car right now would really be more stress than even *she* could handle," I explained.

"Oh! I am *so* embarrassed! Here I am going on about how you should get a car," Shayla said, apologetically. "Is her cancer the genetic kind? Like, do you have to worry about getting it someday, too?" she asked in a quiet way that made me feel all right about discussing it with her.

"We don't know yet," I admitted. "I got my height and my passion for animals from my dad, but I'm hoping my mom just passed on her insane need to succeed and not the cancer gene."

Shayla nodded. "I got my eyes and my laugh from my mom, but I hope I didn't inherit her tendency to wrinkle."

While I considered these things, she dug through one of her bags, pulled out her portfolio, and plunked herself down on the bed beside me. "Want to see my book?"

She phrased it like a question, but the way she pushed her portfolio into my hands said I didn't have a choice.

Shayla's portfolio was thick, and when I took it from her, I was surprised to realize that it was almost as heavy as some of the small dogs we had at the shelter. She looked over my shoulder and narrated as I flipped through photo after photo. There were shots of Shayla in dark rooms, wearing designer clothes, lit up only from one direction. There were pictures of her modeling workout wear in yoga poses that showed off her lean body and there were lingerie shots that made her seem a lot older.

- Posing as Ashley -

I'd been told that the convention was a possible route to bigger agencies and more work than you could get with smaller local places like Gabriella's, but even though I'd only turned a few pages in her portfolio, it seemed to me as if Shayla had already done a lot of cool jobs. Just as I'd had trouble believing my own portfolio shots were really me, I caught myself glancing quickly back at Shayla every once in a while, trying to reconcile the girl beside me with the woman she seemed to become in all of her photographs.

The catalogue work was interesting, but when I saw that some of her stock photography had ended up on the covers of a couple of teen novels, I couldn't hide my jealousy.

"That's you on the cover of these books? That is *so* cool!" I exclaimed with a mixture of excitement and envy. "Were they any good?"

"The books? I don't really know," she said. "I never read them."

"You never read them?" I wouldn't have been able to resist.

"No," she said with a shake of her head. "I think it would be freaky to read a book that's supposed to be about someone else, but has me on the front. I'd be picturing myself all the way through the action," she laughed.

I laughed back, but it came out nervously, because I was feeling intimidated by all of her experience. I hoped Shayla didn't recognize it for what it was. I'd felt so overwhelmed just seeing my basic portfolio shots, I couldn't imagine having a whole book full of professional work.

I was about to discover that the girl who was shoving her portfolio at me actually had very little to do with the smiling girl pictured on its pages.

# CHAPTER 15

To my surprise, at the back of Shayla's portfolio I discovered a program from the last convention. I hadn't realized she'd attended before, and I wondered why she'd come back.

"You competed last year too?" I asked.

"Yeah – first runner-up in photography," she said.

"Wow. You did well," I said, genuinely impressed.

"*Well?* Not exactly!" She slammed her book shut and tossed it on the desk beside her. "I didn't get signed by anyone. You know what the big agencies told me last year? They said I had *potential*. I've been modeling practically my whole life. I should have a lot more than just *potential* at this point – I should have made it by now." Her smile was gone, and her body was tense. She continued in a voice that was tight and clipped.

"*Anyhow,*" she said. "I grew another inch this year, so the European agencies should take me a little more seriously. Did you know that five-foot eight is the absolute minimum height they'll look at in Europe now?"

I nodded my head, remembering that Gabriella had said that even at 5'9", I was probably shorter than they'd want. "I did hear that. How tall are you?"

"Five-eight-and-a-quarter. Standing very straight," she said. Then her mood seemed to get business-like as she asked to see *my* portfolio.

"I only have six pictures," I said apologetically, handing it to her. "Gabriella helped me arrange the shoot at the last minute after she recommended that I attend."

"You haven't actually done any modeling then?" she asked.

"No, none at all." I shook my head, hoping she'd see my potential – the way Gabriella had – and not think I was crazy to have come to a convention so early in what I hoped would be my modeling career. "I'm actually planning to be a veterinarian someday, but the modeling thing just kind of came up. So I thought it would be fun to try."

"I think you'll find it's a lot more *work* than *fun*," she said. Then, unconvincingly, she added, "Your pictures are nice, though." She closed the book quickly and handed it back to me without further comment.

Later, I studied myself in the mirror while I did my make-up for the swimsuit competition. I wasn't trying to see the positives in my appearance that Gabriella had mentioned. I was trying to figure out what my deficits might be: the ones I could in no way compensate for during the competition.

I'd noticed when she'd opened the door that Shayla's towel-wrapped body was willowy and thin. I wondered if the shape of my own, more athletic, body would prove to be a disadvantage for me, the way Shayla's height had proven to be to her disadvantage.

I also worried about my no-color eyes. They're not blue like a *Barbie* doll's, or chocolatey brown, like my mom's. They're not even green, like a cat's, even though Gabriella had described them that way. Really, they're just hazel: green and brown mixed up together. Frog colored.

And as I pulled on my sleek new bathing suit, I wondered again whether I should have had my legs professionally waxed. I'd splurged on one of the new four-bladed razors and shaved my legs and underarms super carefully. There was no visible re-growth, but I could *feel* some.

In retrospect, I probably should have just sucked up the pain of waxing and tried it for my legs, at least. Lots of models, I'd read, get a full Brazilian wax, too, so that their bathing suits and lingerie will sit perfectly smoothly. It *had* to hurt like crazy to have your hair pulled out *down there*! Plus, there would be the added humiliation of spending an afternoon with a stranger at a salon working away at your private areas. That was something I was definitely *not* ready for.

When I went back out to the bedroom, I found Shayla rifling through her beagle-sized make-up bag. She surprised me by pulling out a roll of silver duct tape.

"Can you help me for a minute? I need you to tape up my boobs for the swimsuit comp," she said, heading back into the bathroom and motioning for me to follow.

"Really?" In all of my research, I hadn't read anything about duct tape.

Pulling down the top of her swimsuit to expose her

breasts, she tore off some pieces of the tape, pressed the sticky side against a towel a couple of times, and explained: "I'm going to squeeze my boobs together, and I need you to tape them underneath, so that you can't see it when I put my bathing suit on, okay?"

"Does this actually work?" I asked, wondering why Gabriella hadn't given me this tip.

"Yup. It's like a push-up bra. It makes cleavage, and that's a real boost for the bathing suit competition – pun totally intended. You read the rules, so you know there's no padding allowed, but tape's all right – and nobody will know. If you want, I'll do yours for you after. Just make sure it doesn't show, okay?"

She stuck one end of the tape onto the side of the counter, then grabbed her breasts and squeezed them together. I put four pieces of the thick duct tape underneath them, like she told me, hardly believing how casual some people – okay, specifically, *Shayla* – could be about nudity.

Then she ripped off two short pieces of tape, pressed them into the towel, and stuck them over her nipples.

"So they won't stick out if I get cold," she explained.

When she pulled on her bathing suit, the result was sensational. She'd been transformed from "proportionately endowed" to "noticeably cleavaged."

"Don't stand there gawking," she teased. Then, grabbing the roll of tape, she added, "Do you want me to do yours?"

As I pulled down the top of bathing suit, I thought first of the way the stylist and the photographer at my portfolio shoot had pretty much called me flat-chested, and I hoped Shayla wasn't having the same reaction (which, I knew, was ridiculous, since the whole idea of taping them together was to make them look *bigger*). Then, I thought guiltily about all the appointments my mom had been to and how she'd had to expose herself over and over to the doctors. She had joked to me that it didn't even feel like it mattered anymore whether she covered up her breasts or not.

I also thought about how she had already lost a piece of one breast and seemed only a little bit bothered by it. I was whole and firm and still trying to augment what I had. If I didn't think I was good enough intact, what did that say about my mother, who'd been damaged?

I didn't take it lightly, but I also knew that if I wasn't careful I'd end up obsessing over it all night, so I made a little joke, to lift my mood.

"You know, my boyfriend and I had been together for almost a year before I let him get this far with me," I laughed.

"That's a long time with one guy!" Shayla exclaimed, ripping the tape off quickly with her teeth and sticking it under my breasts without a hint of embarrassment. I tried to look away, but the bathroom had so many mirrors in it, the only way to avoid *seeing* the awkward moment was to close my eyes. And *that* would have made me look weird.

"We went out for two years, actually," I explained, wishing she'd hurry, and still trying to find a good place to look.

"Wow – he must have been pretty great," she said, slapping the two smaller pieces of tape over my nipples.

"He *was* great. His name is Brandon," I told her –
surprised to hear myself reaching a new point, where I could,
in retrospect and without bitterness, call him "great." I
wriggled back into my bathing suit as fast as I could, already
wanting to forget the whole duct taping episode. "I broke up
with him at the beginning of the summer."

"How come you broke up after two whole years?"

I shrugged. "We just wanted different things." To
myself, I thought, "Like *he* wanted to be single, and *I* didn't."
But Brandon wasn't the most important thing in my life
anymore. I didn't want to rehash the break-up *again* at that
moment. I took a deep breath to re-focus, and I stood back to
look in the mirror.

"God! Look at you!" Shayla said as she checked out
her work.

"What?" I asked. "Is the tape showing? Does it look
too fake?"

"No..." she shook her head and looked at me up and
down, the way my mother looks at me when she doesn't like
what I'm wearing. "You look great. You're going to be tougher
competition for me than I thought. Maybe I should keep my
little tricks to myself, huh?"

My question about "fakeness" was not meant to make
Shayla compliment me, but still, I was happy that she had. I
was constantly questioning myself, but I tried not to be the
kind of girl who constantly needs the overt reassurance of
someone else and keeps saying negative things about herself
just so other people will boost her up.

We did look good. It made me feel more confident to see that I wasn't as entirely out of place as I'd initially felt. Shayla wore a lacy black bikini which made her look as if she'd just stepped out of a lingerie ad, and I wore my sexy new red suit.

My glee was short-lived as Shayla pointed at the faint yellow splotches still showing through on my hip. I'd *thought* I'd covered them up well enough with concealer. "Where did you get those bruises?" she asked.

I explained to her about falling down because of the untrained dogs at the shelter, but I didn't want her to think I was a total loser, so I left out the part about practicing my walk.

"That's cool that you work with animals," she said approvingly. "But maybe try to keep your hand low, on your hip, when you walk past the judges."

Already, I understood why Gabriella had thought she'd be a good roommate for me.

When we arrived downstairs a few minutes later for the bathing suit competition, I saw that even the thinnest girls – and some of them were really, really skinny – seemed to have fuller chests than I would have expected on their body types. Obviously a lot of them were taped up like Shayla and me. I also wondered whether one or two of the girls might have been surgically enhanced. On some of the younger girls, I honestly thought it looked unnatural, but that was up to the judges to decide.

As I took my place in line for my first event, I *thought* I was ready for it all.

# CHAPTER 16

Nothing I'd done before the convention had prepared me for the vulnerability I felt as I compared myself to the other girls around me.

Everyone had an assigned order for events, and I ended up in front of a girl named Chelsea. Even though we were inside, she had a pair of dark glasses nestled in the thick red curls on top of her head. She had long legs and big breasts that probably would have looked large even without any tape. I wasn't usually prone to jealousy, and although I always wanted to do my *personal* best, I didn't usually feel competitive toward other people. Standing in front of Chelsea, however, I felt a strange mixture of admiration and intimidation for the second time that day.

I was wondering about my chances alongside all the other girls when a tall woman in a silk blouse, pencil skirt, and sling-backs came out of the competition room to make an announcement.

"The judges will be seeing you individually, in numerical order," she said. "When I nod at you, you are to enter the room through these doors, stop in front of the

judging table, and state your first name, age, and height. You
will exit on the far side of the room. Remember: no pantyhose,
shoes, or props. You must be barefoot. Good luck." And then
she was gone.

"I hope we don't have to wait very long," I said to Chelsea.

"Oh, we probably will."

"*Great*. I hate standing around. I always need to be *doing*
something. I have to pee, too."

"Modeling is always like that, though, isn't it?" Chelsea
said, and I hoped it was a good sign that I was coming across as
someone experienced enough to know what she meant. "I did
a photo shoot for a bridal magazine last month and even
though it took them all day to do my hair and make-up and get
the lighting just right, I felt like a total princess and the photos
were spectacular. I'll show you my book later, if you want."

"Were you in a bridesmaid's dress or something?" I asked.

"Oh no – I was the bride."

*That* seemed crazy.

"How old are you?" I asked.

"Fourteen."

"Seriously? I've heard about them making girls look a
bit older than they really are, but that's *so* young to pose as a
bride!" I said. "Why wouldn't they use someone else?"

"I looked much older by the time they'd done the whole
thing," she said, sounding insulted, and I was sorry I'd said
anything. I hadn't meant to hurt her feelings.

"It's actually standard practice to use younger girls and
make them look older," she explained. "See that girl, Madison

over there? In the silver bathing suit? She's thirteen and she just did a fashion shoot for a major designer. He paid to have her braces removed for the day, while they shot the ad and did a press conference to introduce her as their new 'face,' and then she had the braces put back on again after. She looks about twenty-five in the pictures."

"They actually took her braces *off* for the pictures and then put them back *on*?"

"Yup." Obviously, they couldn't digitally re-touch her teeth at a press conference, but I couldn't imagine how expensive the whole exercise would have been, *or* why an advertiser would even bother. There *had* to be girls the right age, without braces, to do the jobs.

For the next forty minutes, while we waited, Chelsea told me horror story after horror story about modeling. She told one long story about her sister who'd been hired for a job and then was told by the client to get a tan, lighten her hair, and wear tinted contact lenses. I didn't know if she was trying to impress me with her "inside knowledge" or scare me off.

"So maybe models are like boyfriends," I said, trying to sum up her story. "No matter how perfect they seem, there's always *something* you want to change." *Like the fact that they don't want to go out with you anymore*, I thought to myself. She looked at me blankly, and I realized that at fourteen, she might not have been in a serious relationship yet, despite the fact that she'd already played a bride.

It was at that point that the line finally reached the door, and I was about to be in front of the lady in the sling-backs.

Gabriella had warned me that the judges would look at me without expression, but she told me that this didn't mean they disliked me.

In theory, all I had to do was walk in, tell them my name, age, and height, turn around, and leave. But wearing a bathing suit and walking into a room full of people who were fully dressed, and who were essentially there to look me over and find my flaws, was a lot harder than I thought it would be.

I ignored how badly I had to go to the bathroom, tried not to think about the ache in my breasts, and stepped confidently up to the judges table. "I'm sixteen, and I'm five-foot-nine," I said.

A white-haired lady looked at me over the top of her glasses and pursed her lips like a goldfish. "And your *name* is ...?" she asked.

*Dumb!* I'd only had three things to remember, and I'd forgot my own name! I couldn't believe it.

"Ashley," I said in a way that I hoped was bright and memorable. The bald man whispered something to the guy beside him. He then just scribbled something down in a notebook. The lady with the glasses said, "Thank you, Ashley," and nodded in my direction.

Realizing that my turn was over and I'd forgotten something as simple as who I was made me start breathing faster. I had to consciously slow down my breath, thank them, and then walk across the room. This, I did with as much dignity as I could muster. Then I spent the entire elevator ride up to my floor berating myself for messing up.

I zipped past Shayla and into the bathroom as soon as I got to the room. When I came back out, she was flopped down on my bed, which, as an only child and a control freak, bugged me. I knew my reaction was stupid, so I tried not to let it show.

"How'd it go?" she asked.

"Let's just say it's a good thing I'm not here to do rocket science," I said, still feeling like an idiot, "because once I got in there I forgot to give them my name!"

Laughing, she said, "For swimsuit they just look at your body. Nothing else counts. It doesn't matter if you're an opera singer or a brain surgeon, as long as you fill out the suit. The acting portion, for commercials, is where you want to make sure you're really poised." I wished I could have checked with Gabriella, to make sure I hadn't already blown everything, but I didn't know how to do it without drawing attention to our connection. Besides, I was still reluctant to keep bugging her with stupid questions.

I couldn't wait to get out of my bathing suit, but even though I'd taped Shayla's breasts, and she'd taped mine, I felt self-conscious, so I turned away from her to change. The tape really stung as I attempted to pull it off. It was like tearing off a huge bandage, only the skin on my breasts was a lot more tender than any place I'd ever needed a bandage before.

"It hurts a lot less if you just rip it right off," Shayla interjected from the other side of the room.

Gritting my teeth, I yanked it off. "OOWW!" I howled. "I think I might have actually torn off some skin!"

"It shouldn't be that bad," she said. "That's why we

pressed it against the towel before we put it on – so it wouldn't stick quite so much."

I thought back to the scene in the bathroom. I remembered Shayla doing the towel thing with the tape I'd used on her, but by the time she did mine, I was averting my eyes and talking about Brandon. I couldn't remember whether she'd actually pressed it into the towel first or not.

I looked down as I pulled on my bra and saw that there were bright red marks crisscrossing under my breasts like a roadmap, where the tape had been. Again, I began to think about my mom, but Shayla interrupted my thoughts.

"There's a party upstairs tonight," she said. "Want to come?"

"I don't know. I have to find some dinner somewhere, and I don't want to end up too tired and have circles under my eyes tomorrow morning."

"Is that you talking, or your mother?" she asked. She'd obviously already caught on to my "please the parents" side.

"A little of both," I admitted with a giggle. "They have me pretty well-trained."

"Oh – come on – just for a little while. All the guys here are really hot," she said. "And I already ordered a pizza for dinner. The rest of it is over there," she motioned to the desk. "You should have the leftovers. I made the mistake of going to *last year's* party on an empty stomach."

The shadow of missing Brandon had started sneaking up on me again when she'd mentioned all the guys who would be there. Knowing it would be easier not to think about him if I was busy, I agreed to go to the party after I'd eaten and then fixed myself up.

Normally, re-touching my make-up would have calmed me down, but even as I added some blush and a little more eyeliner, I couldn't stop thinking about how stupid I'd sounded in front of the judges, and how I needed to be better prepared for the next event.

My mom's phone went straight to voicemail when I tried her, so I left a quick message that I hoped didn't reveal my frustration. Then I called Caitlyn while I nibbled on cold pizza.

"I'm going up to a party with a bunch of male models," I told her, after I'd filled her in on the swimsuit competition.

"Oh, Ashley – that's great! Go have an amazing time. You haven't been single for two years … this is going to be like a brand new box of paints when all you've ever had are a couple of crayons!"

"I'm not feeling very artistic," I whined, just a little, over her metaphor.

"Okay, but maybe just go check out the hot new colors," she teased.

# CHAPTER 17

I thought about Caitlyn's encouragement on my way up to the party. When I arrived, I recognized a few of the girls from the swimsuit competition sitting cross-legged on the carpet, drinks in hand, flirting with guys who were obviously there as competitors as well. The funny thing was, it looked just like any other party at home, but with taller attendees. People were dressed pretty normally, and their hair and make-up weren't overdone. I'd forgotten that most of the other competitors were just regular high school kids like me.

The heat and cigarette smoke made me gag as soon as I walked in. With the door to the balcony open for the smokers, the air conditioner had cut out and with no place else to go, the smoke had clogged up the room.

Having spent the whole day in air conditioning, I hadn't realized how hot and muggy it was outside. And my sense of balance felt off, which made me even dizzier. I'm used to being the tallest girl in the room, and often the guys are even smaller than me, but walking in there made me feel like a little kid again. I had to look up – literally – to so many people.

"Ashley!"

I turned around, grateful to hear a familiar voice, just as Shayla was coming around the corner with a tall brunette in a tight white dress.

Shayla rushed over and put her arm around my shoulder, leading me to her friend.

"Ashley!" she said again. "I've been waiting for you! This is Grace, one of my best friends. Grace, this is Ashley, my roommate. Gabriella found her. Isn't she gorgeous? I told you she was going to mean some serious competition this year."

When she got to the "isn't she gorgeous" part, she grabbed my face between her hands – the way grandmothers do on T.V. sitcoms, and I had to fight off the urge to swat her away.

Grace came forward. "Hey. It's nice to meet you," she said. "Shayla, let go of the poor girl."

Grace had long, thick hair, like mine, and dark eyes. Her skin glowed.

"Do you want a beer?" she asked, motioning toward a cooler.

"No thanks," I said, shaking my head. "I don't want to be all bloated and gassy for the competition tomorrow."

"See? Beautiful AND smart!" Shayla said, as she handed me some bottled water.

I've never actually had a beer. It wasn't as if I'd never been offered one before, but I'd discovered long ago that when I was around other people who were drinking, I could usually make a joke or an excuse – like the gas thing. As long as I was confident about it, they usually let me off the hook without too much trouble. I was happy that it seemed to have worked this time, too, because even though I was away from parental scrutiny, I was too much of a worrier, like my mom, to start drinking for the first time on a night when I had to be awake and alert the next day.

I stood with Grace and Shayla, getting the scoop on some of the other people in the room and wondering what those people were saying about us.

"Check out Brooke's new hair extensions," Grace said, motioning toward a girl with blond hair almost to her waist.

"I knew she hadn't grown it out that fast," Shayla commented. "It was barely down to her shoulders last fall."

"And it's going to be short again," Grace said. "The extensions are too heavy, and she's got all these little bald patches underneath where they're glued on. She showed me earlier."

"Bald patches?" Shayla exclaimed. "Did she go to a cheap salon or what?"

"No – one of the clients had them put in for some show she did," Grace said. "She told me her own hairdresser said they were just too heavy for her hair, so she's only keeping them in for this weekend."

"That's so nasty!" Shayla said, squishing up her nose.

"You know what else is nasty? I don't think I got all the butt glue off when I showered – my thong's sticking to me!" She turned her head and reached around to adjust her dress.

Shayla must have noticed the look of horror on my face because she quickly offered an explanation. "She means *body adhesive.* Some of the girls like to make sure their bikinis don't ride up too far during swimsuit." She made a face at Grace. "But the smart ones wash it all off!"

"How do you guys learn about all these little tricks?" I asked wondering why Gabriella hadn't mentioned them, but knowing it might have made me more nervous if she had.

Shayla shrugged. "It's just common industry knowledge … they do the same stuff when we're in photo shoots and fashion shows. We just bring it back to the real world."

"At the very least, you must know about putting Vaseline on your teeth, right?" Grace asked me. "It reminds you to smile – because it tastes disgusting when you close your lips. Plus, when you do smile, it makes your teeth look shiny, and it keeps your mouth from drying out."

I made a face at the thought of it, and Shayla leaned in, as if she was going to tell me a secret. "It's gross, but I'm so used it that I started kissing a guy one time before I realized I hadn't wiped it off."

"You have such a one-track mind, Shayla," Grace squealed, before turning back to me.

"Oh … I don't think I'd want to use Vaseline," I said. "I just read that over a lifetime, the average woman probably swallows about five pounds of lipstick already."

Shayla cut me off as she burst out laughing. "I wonder how much lipstick the average boyfriend swallows!"

"See what I mean?" Grace asked me in mock exasperation. "She has boys on the brain."

"Hey, no more than you, Miss 'Adjust-my-thong-in-public'!" Shayla told her. "Anyway, we need to get Ashley hooked up tonight. She just broke up with someone and she needs to get back in the game."

"Oooh – you came to the right place," Grace said, looking around. "There are some definite hotties here this year."

"Yeah, but sadly, the girls are all pretty hot, too," I said, surveying the others.

"At least when you meet someone at one of these events, you know they're not just after your looks," Grace said.

Shayla snorted. "It's ALL about the looks."

"Yeah, but it's not like at school, where they just want to say they're with a model. Here it's more like a level playing field – competition-wise – so at least there's a bit of fun in the chase."

"Yeah. There's more challenge here, for sure," Shayla giggled. "And more reward."

"You saw Justin, right?" Grace asked Shayla, suddenly ignoring me.

"We said 'hi'," she said coolly. I could tell there was more to it than she was letting on, but I knew from personal experience that sometimes you just don't want to get into all the details, so I didn't ask.

"You know what?" I said. "I don't actually feel that great. Maybe I'll go see if there's any room on the balcony. I think I need some fresh air."

"Maybe you swallowed too much lipstick this afternoon!" Shayla called after me.

"I hear it's very fattening!" Grace added, laughing.

I worked my way out to the balcony, and leaned against the rail. It was warm outside, but not as stuffy as in the room.

A blond guy with blue eyes came up behind me and leaned on the railing next to me.

"Is this spot taken?" the gorgeous guy asked.

"I've been off the market for a long time, but I'm pretty sure that line went out years ago," I said before introducing myself.

"I'm Justin," he said with a friendly smile. "It's nice to meet you, Ashley." If his flawless looks and cheesy line hadn't already caught my attention, hearing the name Grace had mentioned *would* have.

# CHAPTER 18

"Did you say *Justin*? I think I might have just heard someone talking about you," I said, and then stopped. I realized he'd want more specifics, which I couldn't provide. It really wasn't any of my business.

"Uh-oh. Whatever it was, I didn't do it," he joked. "Unless you were here last year. In which case you probably think I'm lying."

"I'm a newbie," I said, wondering what he meant by his last comment.

"Are you? This is my second year. I'm either determined or a complete sucker for rejection."

"My mother would love you – she's totally into never giving up," I told him. Then I panicked, realizing he probably thought I wanted to take him home to meet her.

Thankfully, he seemed to still be thinking about the first thing I'd said and he missed the "mother" reference completely. "So ... what did you hear about me?"

I tried again to get myself off the hook. "Nothing – I just overheard someone say they said 'hi' to Justin."

"Well, I *am* a pretty popular guy," he said jokingly. Some

people behind us, who had obviously been drinking, started singing the K-I-S-S-I-N-G song, and when they stopped, Justin leaned in a little closer and continued. "So, Newbie – how are you finding it here?"

I looked around, thinking carefully before I answered. "It's different from how I thought it would be," I admitted. "I'm not really like the other girls here. I feel like I'm only posing as one of them," I said. "You?"

He grinned. "I'm not really like the other girls here, either." He continued, leaning in again and whispering so close to my ear that I caught a whiff of his cologne. "I don't really like wearing make-up."

It felt good to finally meet someone at the convention who was so unlike me and didn't take themselves too seriously. I laughed. "You know, normally I would respond to that with a really interesting factoid, but it just fell flat in there," I said as I pointed to the room.

"I don't believe you. *Everyone* loves a good factoid. Try me." We'd been leaning over the balcony, side by side, staring out at the parking lot. But now he put his hands on my shoulders and gently turned me around to face him. He was so smooth about it that I was almost disappointed when he let go of me.

"It was just that I read that an average woman could swallow up to five pounds of lipstick in her lifetime. And now I'm wondering how much that would mean male models swallow, during their careers."

"I heard this one!" his eyes opened wide and he pointed

his index finger up toward the sky while he thought. "And somebody else calculated that five pounds is something like a hundred tubes of lipstick, which most people would probably never own, so even guys like me who get all gussied up for the camera don't actually have to worry about lipstick poisoning!" He looked mischievous as he tucked a loose strand of my hair behind my ear. I felt a shiver down my back when he touched me again, and I tried to work out in my brain whether I was reacting to his touch, or to his good looks, or to the fact that he'd liked my factoid.

A few minutes later, I decided it had to be his personality. He told me that he planned to be a lawyer, and then he listened with interest as I told him about working at the animal shelter and about my plans to be a vet.

"My dog was a rescue," he said. I instantly liked him even more. "His name is Bo. He's a black and white cross between a Border Collie and a Lab,"

I thought for a second about the combination. "So, that makes him a *Blab*," I told him. "Or a *Lollie-pup!*"

"Ha, you're quick," he said, and I was proud that he thought so. "I've had him for three years, and neither one of those names had ever occurred to me. Either way, though, he's awesome," he said. "He's so smart and he never seems to slow down. He's happiest when he has something to do."

"That's what the breed is like," I said, secretly delighted that he was a Border Collie kind of guy. When he slid his hand down onto mine and held it, I told myself that maybe "seeing other people" wouldn't be quite as bad as I'd anticipated.

Someone had cranked up the music and the balcony was more crowded than when I'd first arrived. Plus, the night seemed to be getting muggier. Physically, I was starting to feel sick again, but Justin seemed to be enjoying my quirky facts, and I was enjoying his presence – both of which made me reluctant to leave.

"This is going to sound like I'm totally trying to blow you off," I said carefully after a few minutes, hoping he wouldn't take it that way, "but I actually came out here originally because I wasn't feeling very well. I think I need to head back to my room and get some sleep."

"Do you want me to walk you back?" he asked. "Just to make sure you get there okay?"

"I'm all right – it's only a couple of floors."

"Yeah, but there could be a lot of creeps out there," Justin said in a silly – but sinister – voice.

"How do I know *you're* not a creep?" I asked.

He shrugged. "You don't, I guess. But if anything *did* happen to you, I'd likely be the prime suspect, since I'll have been the last one anybody saw you with. So you might as well let me walk you down, and then at least *I'll* know you got there safely." He was going to make a very good lawyer.

I agreed, and he came with me out to the elevator, and back to my door.

"So, you're really not trying to get away from me?" he asked.

"I'm really not." I remembered how Gabriella had asked my dad out, and just then I decided to go for it myself. "Maybe

I could track you down after the competitions tomorrow? Like, three o'clock? At the restaurant in the lobby?"

"Cool. So, if we're going to see each other tomorrow, would it be okay if I gave you a quick hug goodnight?"

"Okay..."

He leaned against the door as we hugged and he spoke very quietly. "And it would be okay if I gave you just the tiniest goodnight kiss?"

I nodded, but said nothing. It had been a long time since I'd had a crush on anyone new, and the courage I'd felt in asking him out had suddenly melted into a total inability to speak.

After two years of kissing only one guy, I still felt slightly disloyal when Justin's lips touched mine, even though Brandon and I had been broken up for three weeks now. But that feeling passed as I kissed him more deeply and realized that despite the way I tried to plan everything, right at that moment, it felt good to be a little bit impulsive.

Before I knew it, we were making out in the hall.

Brandon had been my first serious boyfriend, and since we were so young when we started going out, everything had been built up over a period of months and even years – the first kiss, the first time he touched my bra, the first time he took it off. And yet with Justin, it was almost as if we started out right where Brandon and I had left off. His kiss made me shiver all the way down my back in a way Brandon's hadn't, though I didn't know at the time what I was missing. And although it felt daring to let a guy I'd just met work his hand up my back and under my shirt – and I remembered teasing Caitlyn just a year ago, when her new boyfriend had done the same thing! – it wasn't the huge deal I might have expected since I'd already crossed that threshold of letting someone up there.

"Get a room!" someone called out, joking, as we stood there, kissing against the doorway.

The taunting jarred me back to reality, and I felt embarrassed by how far things had gotten in such a public space, with a guy I'd just met. "I can't let you in there," I whispered, motioning toward the door with my head.

"You have good instincts," he said. "Because I don't really trust myself right now, either."

"I have to go get some sleep so I don't mess everything up tomorrow," I said, not totally believing it myself.

He kissed me again, lightly, on the mouth. "That's okay, I'll see you tomorrow, right? In the restaurant, around three?"

I nodded and committed the time to memory.

"Before you go, tell me a little factoid about yourself," I said, wanting a detail I could hold onto.

"Like what?"

"I don't know ... what's *your* deepest, darkest secret?" I whispered.

"Deep, dark secret? Okay – I wasn't planning on meeting anyone special this weekend, but there's just something about you ..."

It wasn't the kind of personal detail I'd been looking for, but still, it made me happy. I kissed him softly.

"What's your deepest, darkest secret?" he asked.

"I never feel like I'm good enough at anything I do."

Case in point: as soon as I'd said it, I felt as if I'd actually messed up the moment, because Justin raised his eyebrows in mock astonishment. I worried that I'd gotten too deep and had shown too much vulnerability to someone I'd just met. I pulled away from him. "But that information's protected by lawyer/client privilege, right?" I added, furious at myself for admitting to it, even in a joking way.

Shayla came around the corner just then. Her eyes opened wide when she saw us, then locked with Justin's.

"I see you two have met," she said icily. Although she hadn't been drinking anything when I'd been talking to her earlier, it was obvious from the way she sounded that she'd had something afterward. "Is he still a good kisser, Ashley?" she crossed her arms and leaned against the wall.

I looked quickly at Justin to gauge his reaction, but his face didn't reveal anything one way or another.

"You look ... as good as last year, Shayla," he said.

"I'll take that as a compliment," she retorted, lifting her chin a bit higher. "Look out for him," she warned me. "He went after my roommate last year, too."

"Which is how she's heard about my kissing," Justin explained quickly, while I wondered why Shayla was trying to make me think otherwise. "But thanks for spreading the word, Shayla." He turned back to me to me. "I'd better take off. I'll find you tomorrow?"

I nodded, embarrassed that Shayla had found us making out in the hall, and relieved that Gabriella hadn't come by at all.

"What was that about?" I asked Shayla when we got into the room.

She shrugged, as if it was nothing, but I knew there was more to it. "Like I said – he went after my roommate last year, that's all."

She shut herself in the bathroom without saying anything else, and I was left to wonder what was going on. I texted Caitlyn quickly – to tell her I'd "put some paint on my palette" – before wiping my make-up off and crawling into bed.

# CHAPTER 19

I fell asleep right away that night and slept soundly. But when I woke up the next morning, I was anxious about the day ahead – and I was starving for some real food. I hadn't actually eaten much of the pizza, and I figured that my light-headedness at the party, and my impulsiveness with Justin, had something to do with not having eaten a decent dinner.

Either way, I needed food. Shayla was still sound asleep and would likely wake up with a headache, so I dressed quickly and went downstairs on my own.

Gabriella approached me as I was grabbing yogurt, fruit, and a couple of muffins from the Continental breakfast in the lobby. It was comforting to see a familiar face.

"Hi, Ashley! How are things going?" she asked with her usual enthusiasm. I told her about forgetting my name at the swimsuit competition, and I felt a huge sense of relief when she agreed that although it had *seemed* pathetic to me, the judges probably wouldn't have even noticed or cared.

"I also heard that you and Justin really seemed to hit it off," she teased.

Knowing how quickly stories spread, I guess I shouldn't

have been surprised that Gabriella had heard from someone about my public display of affection. But I wondered whether she'd *heard* about it, or if maybe she'd come by looking for me and seen it for herself. I felt a strange combination of pleasure and embarrassment remembering our make-out session in the hall, but I hoped she wouldn't report back to my parents about it. "Yeah, I don't know what came over me. I don't usually kiss people I meet at parties. Remember, I went out with one guy for two years."

Mercifully, she didn't press for more details. "I know, but you look kind of tired. Maybe you should have gone to bed a bit earlier – or slept in," she said.

"Thanks for the vote of confidence."

"You're ready – you'll be fine," she reassured me and laughed a little.

I wasn't so certain myself. I'd forgotten who I was.

"There is one thing I was thinking about, though," she said. "I know you practiced that 'Cat's Pyjamas' ad – and it was cute – but I heard some of the judges talking about last year's commercials, and it seems that they actually find it easier to judge something they're already familiar with. I probably shouldn't even be telling you this … still, there's no rule saying you have to be original, so I'm thinking we might want to switch your routine to a commercial that's already out there."

I felt my jaw tighten at the thought of coming up with something at the last minute, and my instincts told me that I'd be better off sticking to what I'd prepared. But Gabriella was the expert and she had "inside knowledge." Plus, I'd promised to trust her judgment.

"Did you have one in mind – one that I might know?" I asked hopefully.

"I do, actually – that lingerie commercial – you know, the one that's on all the time now, with the woman who talks about having her own little secret, and you think it's going to be an affair, but then it turns out it's just that she's wearing nice undies?"

I did know it. And thinking about it, my own Cat's Pyjamas ad seemed stupid and immature. It occurred to me that besides doing something familiar to the judges, maybe I also needed to do something more grown up, too.

I remembered lines from the ad very clearly because they were clever. I went over them in my mind all morning as I prepared for the day ahead. I thought about the ad while I was doing my hair, my make-up, and while I was getting dressed.

As I pulled out my new black dress, I knew that Caitlyn hadn't steered me wrong – it *was* perfect. I'd also bought new underwear to put underneath. Not just regular everyday cotton underwear, but soft, lacy lingerie made out of light purple silk. Even if I'm the only one who knows about it, I like having my bra and panties match. It always makes me feel more put together, which makes me feel more confident. Having my own new things also helped me get into the right mindset for the specific lingerie commercial Gabriella had recommended I try.

Shayla was wearing a black bodysuit with footless tights, ballet flats, and a short black skirt over the tights.

Everything was very form-fitting. She'd blow-dried her hair super straight and swept her long bangs partly across her face. Her make-up was very dramatic: she had dark black liner all the way around her eyes, false eyelashes, and shimmering red lipstick.

She actually looked as if she'd just stepped out of a fashion magazine.

"You ready?" she asked.

"I need to use the bathroom before I go downstairs this time," I said. "You can go ahead."

"I'll wait for you," Shayla said. "I want to throw together an emergency kit to take down anyway."

"What's in your emergency kit?" I asked, looking at the large leather bag she was carrying.

"Lipstick, safety pins, stain remover – stuff like that," she said with a shrug.

Shayla grabbed what she needed while I finished up, and we headed downstairs together for the runway competition.

Even before I got down there to take my place in line, I saw that Chelsea had gone with the white option and was wearing a wedding dress. Her hair was piled up on top of her head, and her earrings dangled down to her shoulders. When I took my place in front of her, she was trying to figure out where to pin her number without covering her breasts.

"Hey, great dress idea – I never even thought of that!" I said when I saw her. "I wore one of my mom's old wedding dresses for Halloween last year, but it didn't occur to me that I could do it here."

"You can wear whatever you want for runway, as long as it's black or white," she said a little defensively.

"I know ... I read the regulations. I just didn't think about a wedding dress."

"This is the one I wore for the photo shoot last month," she explained.

"They let you keep it?"

"No, but I talked the shop into letting me borrow it for the competition. I really love runway and I wanted something special to wear. I've taken regular *and* advanced classes. I know all the turns. This is my strongest area of competition."

As much as it bugged me, I knew that I didn't have any control over whether or not the other girls had taken advanced runway modeling, or whether they were prettier, or taller, or anything else. But with walking, I was hoping the practice I'd done with Gabriella and Caitlyn would help me *appear* confident, at least a little. And, I was still kind of light-headed from my make-out session with Justin, so I felt like I could float down the catwalk and conquer the competition.

They were letting us in five at a time, so I got to watch a few of the girls ahead of me doing their routines. One of them had trouble moving with the beat of the music, and another one only used two kinds of turns. The girl in front of me was really graceful and made me wonder if she'd had dance training as well.

I was only nervous for a few seconds. As I took my first couple of steps, I reminded myself that I'd practiced hard, and I couldn't do anything more at that moment except demonstrate what I'd learned. That was my last conscious thought before my body took over and led me through an almost-perfect routine.

"You were great in there," Chelsea complimented me afterward. "You looked like you've been doing this forever."

I hoped Chelsea's praise would be echoed by the judges and agents who were watching. Even though Gabriella said she was grooming me more for photography than runway, I was glad I'd put so much work into it. The feeling of having had done my best, and having it turn out well, was both motivating and encouraging.

I didn't have much time to get to the commercial competition, which was next, but somehow, Chelsea had managed to change out of her wedding dress and into a tight spandex top and cycling shorts. The top was divided into different sections of color, with blue on her right breast, and yellow on the left. "I made up a commercial about active wear," she explained.

I had to give her credit – she definitely knew how to choose outfits that left an impression on you.

*My* dress seemed determined to leave an impression, too. It had picked up some static during the runway routine, and was now clinging to my legs. I was fussing with it when Shayla came by. It was almost my turn to go in for the commercial audition.

"I heard your runway went really well," she said. "Congratulations."

"Thanks – I'm going to look like an idiot in there now, though," I said, indicating the room I was about to enter. "My dress is all clingy."

"Wait! I have spray for that in my bag," Shayla said, digging through her emergency kit.

"I don't know if I have time," I said, panicking, because they'd already opened the door.

"Here!" Shayla said, tossing me a spray can. I lifted my skirt and made few quick passes back and forth over my thighs – front and back – before heading in for my acting debut.

Again, we entered the room five at a time. I was the fourth one in our group.

This time, I stated my name and number very clearly, and they started the timer – I was going to have points deducted if I went over the thirty-second mark.

When the judges were quiet, I started my monologue.

"I've got a secret that makes me feel good all over," I whispered in a way that I hoped was sexy. The woman on T.V. who did the actual ad was sort of playful in her delivery, but I was trying to change it, to show that I could be creative. Partway through, when I noticed that the judges were whispering to each other, I started to wonder if the way I was doing it might actually sound kind of raspy and creepy, instead of sexy. Then, I realized that my dress hadn't gotten any better from the spray – in fact, in places, it was actually stuck right to my nylons. Some of the spectators were whispering to each other and pointing in my direction. I felt my face get hot and it was all I could do to keep the last little bit of my dignity intact and finish the monologue without running offstage.

As I finished, the judges gave me confused smiles, and some of the other girls giggled and laughed. Chelsea's eyes grew wide and her whole face lengthened the way Caitlyn's goldfish does when it's gulping air.

My face got hot and I felt really unsteady.

Shayla was waiting for me outside, biting her lower lip.

"I screwed up so bad," she said. "Ashley – I'm sorry – you were in such a hurry to get out there, I didn't grab the anti-static spray."

She didn't have to hold up the can of body adhesive. I'd already figured it out.

"I thought it was the anti-static stuff," she declared. "You were in a huge hurry to get out there and look, they're both spray cans."

I didn't know what to say. I was so embarrassed and confused, I didn't know whether to believe that it was an accident, like she said, or whether she was jealous and still upset about Justin.

Mostly, though, I was disappointed with myself for having needed Shayla's "help" and advice. If I'd just done better research or been less stubborn and asked Gabriella more questions, I could have learned about the tape *and* been prepared for static cling myself.

"Yeah – I guess it's my fault, too, for not looking carefully enough – I have to go change," I mumbled as I wandered away from Shayla.

Chelsea was waiting for the elevator when I got there, and despite my dress disaster she surprised me with a compliment. "I liked how you tried to change the commercial a bit to show your creativity and versatility," she said to me. "It was funny."

I had no idea why she would have thought it was funny, apart from my dress – unless, of course, I'd done something else wrong. I tried to be casual. "My voice sounded weird, though, didn't it?" I watched her expression and saw her blink a few times before she answered.

"No – it sounded good – it was really sultry. It made that switch with the last line even funnier, because it wasn't what you'd expect to hear someone say with a sexy voice like that."

"What switch?" I felt myself starting to shake. The last line was *"Because everyone needs a change."* I didn't know what she was talking about, but I felt my stomach tightening up.

"Where you said, 'Because everyone needs to change their underwear.'"

"What? I said *that*?"

"Didn't you mean to?"

"No! I meant to do the original line … about needing a change. I *never* do stuff like this – ever – I don't know what's wrong with me." I thought I might get sick as I slid down onto the floor. I'd wrecked my speech, and my dress was stuck to my thighs, probably ruined. Feeling defeated, I put my head on my knees. Chelsea squatted down beside me.

"Hey, are you okay?"

"I don't know," I told her. "I'm usually totally prepared, so I don't make mistakes. But I've screwed up two things out of three – or three out of two, if you count swimsuit plus both problems with my monologue," I babbled.

"Do you ... ummm ... want me to get you anything?"

Seeing Chelsea's worried face when I looked up reminded me, for the first time since I'd met her, that she *wasn't* just a body in a bikini or a woman in a wedding dress. She was a fourteen year old girl, playing dress-up in a grown-up world. And she didn't know what to do about sixteen-year-old me, slumped on the floor in front of her.

I smiled to reassure her – and myself – despite the odd looks I was getting as other contestants walked by.

"I'll be okay," I said. "I always am."

# CHAPTER 20

Eventually, I pulled myself up off the floor, so that I could get cleaned up without being late to meet Justin. I was looking forward to seeing him again, and I was happy to have somewhere to hang out besides my hotel room. By the time I'd showered and changed, Shayla hadn't yet returned to the room, which made me wonder if she was avoiding me. A normal person might have viewed her apparent avoidance as evidence of a guilty conscience, but I thought maybe it was somehow all my own fault, for being in such a rush to get into the commercial room.

Justin was already waiting for me at a table near the front of the restaurant. He stood and kissed me lightly on the cheek when I arrived, in a familiar way, as if we'd been a couple forever. As if we *were* a couple. I didn't *think* we were, but I didn't know for sure. As I considered these things, I only picked at the nachos he'd ordered.

"Oh no – not you, too," he said.

"Not me what?"

"Not another model who won't eat anything."

"Oh, I eat," I assured him, relieved that he didn't have

any real criticism. "You should have seen the mammoth muffins I devoured at breakfast." In remembering all the kissing, I'd forgotten how easy he was to talk to.

"*Devoured?*" he raised an eyebrow.

"Yeah – I ate the yogurt and fruit slowly, but the muffin was too good to just nibble." I was sick of small-talk already. "So what's the deal with you and Shayla?" I asked. "She seemed pretty miffed to see you with me last night."

"Yeah – she was snarky *and* smashed," he said.

"I didn't expect to see her come back so tipsy. I hadn't even seen her drinking."

"I wasn't that surprised," he said. "Last year, she got into drinking pretty hard, and her roommate, Cristal, found her passed out on their bathroom floor – beside the toilet."

"Oh my gosh!" It was hard to imagine Shayla lying on a bathroom floor.

"Anyway," he continued. "Cristal couldn't get Shayla up, so she called me to help her."

"Oh wow – no wonder she's uncomfortable around you!" I said. I wasn't quite as uptight as my mom about having perfect hair and make-up, but I definitely wouldn't have wanted anyone to see me passed out like *that*.

"Oh – she's not just *uncomfortable* around me – she's still mad," he said.

"How come?"

"Because we couldn't wake her up – even by putting cold water on her face. It was really scary. Cristal had just wanted to let her sleep it off, but I was afraid she could have alcohol poisoning, so I called 911 and then tried mouth-to-mouth, which is why she jokes about how I kiss – even though she was totally unconscious. They ended up taking her away in an ambulance and she missed the rest of the weekend."

"But she said she was first runner-up in photography last year."

"Besides swimsuit, that was the only part she ended up competing in," he said, "because the judges mainly work from the 8x10s submitted. They don't actually need you to be there for it."

"She never told me any of *that*," I said. "Wow. I had no idea."

"I wouldn't have said anything about it if she hadn't been drinking again last night," he said. "I was so relieved that she had made a full recovery last year – I really hoped she'd learned her lesson. She still seems to be making stupid choices, though, and blaming me for trying to help."

I told him, then, about the butt glue (being careful to actually call it by its proper name), but I left out the duct tape incident because it was totally embarrassing. He agreed with me that it was hard to know whether or not the static spray situation had been intentional or not.

"Still, you might want to steer clear of her, just in case," he said. "Because she seems to be holding a grudge against me, and you may be getting the brunt of it by association."

"How do I avoid her when we're sharing a room?" I asked.

"Well, if you don't have your heart set on going to

another party tonight, I was thinking we could head out and catch a movie down the street," he offered.

It was totally sweet that he wanted to go on a real date, but I hesitated for a second out of habit and tried to calculate the "smart thing to do." Justin reassured me. "Come on," he teased. "We've already kissed, so the least you can do is give me a first date!"

The idea of hanging out with Justin was way more appealing than spending the night at the hotel, trying to avoid Shayla, so I agreed. I made another quick trip back to my room to grab my purse, but Shayla still hadn't returned – or, at least, she wasn't there at that moment. Even though we weren't acknowledging our family connection, I texted Gabriella to let her know I'd be leaving the hotel, just in case she was looking for me.

Then, Justin and I headed out for a couple of hours away from the world of modeling. The movie we saw was totally lame, but he made funny remarks all the way through it, and we laughed a lot together.

Our break from the competition didn't last long. By the time we got back to the hotel later that night, all the awards had been posted in the lobby. Shayla had won the photography competition, and Chelsea had placed first in swimsuit. Neither Justin nor I had placed at all.

I tried to hide my disappointment – which was deep – but Justin saw right through me.

"The awards don't really mean that much," he said. "You can still get a contract – even if you didn't win in any of the categories."

I nodded, knowing he was right, but still wishing I'd had a prize to tell my mom and dad about. At least Gabriella hadn't been there beside me when I saw that I hadn't won. I knew it would be easier to face her once I'd gotten used to the idea of not being picked.

Justin walked me back up to my room and kissed me goodnight – quickly this time. Shayla still hadn't returned – she was likely out partying up her win. I went to bed, exhausted from the mental effort of trying to be on top all the time, without the satisfaction of feeling as if I was accomplishing anything. Surprisingly, I slept soundly all night.

I awoke early in the morning to the ringtone on my cell.

"Ashley!" Gabriella cooed over the phone as I struggled to wake up fully and remember where I was. "Callbacks have already begun in the ballroom. There are several agencies interested in talking to you – and many of them are just *excellent*. I just knew I was right about you."

The tone of her voice told me that she wasn't just saying things she thought I'd want to hear. The wave that came over me then was one of intense relief and satisfaction.

"Can you meet me downstairs in the ballroom in half an hour?" she asked. "Wear light make-up, form-fitting clothes."

Twenty-five minutes later, Gabriella was sitting with me while I spoke to representatives from the interested agencies. She took notes, which was really helpful because I was too excited and overwhelmed trying to compare the different agencies. I knew I'd need a day or two to think about their offers and discuss them with my parents before accepting anything.

"You need to consider all sorts of things," Gabriella explained. "Not just how big or prestigious the agency is. You have to remember that even though the larger companies may have more clients looking for models, they'll also have more girls to send out who will be competing with you for those jobs. And you won't always get the same personal attention from them as you might with a smaller agency.

"Location is also a factor," she continued. "Some of these agencies will expect you to live in the big urban centers. I've met *some* parents who are willing to relocate to support their daughter's career, but because your parents share joint custody, you probably have to rule those offers out right away."

Justin had also been invited back into the ballroom for callbacks, and I ran into him as I was finishing up with Gabriella. He was considering a few offers of his own, but that didn't stop him from being ecstatic for me. "You'll know which one is right for you," he promised, when I told him how overwhelming it was to choose between them. Then he added, "You know, remember the other night, when you said you weren't really like the other girls here?"

It seemed so long ago. "I remember."

"I knew you were right," he said. "You're just as beautiful and determined as everyone else here, but there's also something different about you ... I haven't figured it out yet, but I want to."

For a minute, everything felt as if it was happening to someone else. A year earlier, I'd come down kind of hard on

Caitlyn for making out with a guy she'd just met, even though she wanted to keep seeing him. Now, not only had *I* made out with a guy *I'd* just met, I wasn't sure whether or not I would ever see him again.

Up until the point where he said he wanted to "figure me out," I'd deliberately stopped myself from thinking about what would happen with Justin after the convention. He was great – smart and funny and good-looking – but I hadn't known whether we were just having a little bit of weekend fun, or whether he intended it to be something more. I was too embarrassed to have a big "where are we going" relationship talk two days after I'd met him. We lived more than an hour apart, which meant any relationship we could have would be long-distance. Plus, even though I didn't see myself as a "kiss 'em and leave 'em" kind of girl, I wasn't sure about whether or not I was ready to get into another relationship so soon after Brandon.

I must have looked like an idiot standing there thinking all those things, because he looked kind of shy as he spoke again. "So, do you think we could stay in touch? Maybe get together again later in the summer or something?"

"That would be perfect," I said, liking the way he left the possibility open but not absolute.

The two of us had a late breakfast together after the callbacks, and he walked me to my room. After a bit more kissing, we said goodbye and he left me to pack my things.

I was still thinking about him and the modeling offers when Shayla arrived.

I'd already been asleep the night before when she returned from another party, and she hadn't been up yet when Gabriella had called me that morning, so I still hadn't had a chance to talk to her about the "mix-up" with the static spray.

"I heard you got some good contract offers," she said without even a "Good morning" or a "How are you?"

I didn't know yet if anything had worked out for *her*, so I tried to play down the contracts. "Yeah, I've got some stuff to think about, anyway. It'll depend a bit on my parents."

"So I guess it's okay that I messed up your dress yesterday. I mean, it didn't hurt your presentation, obviously." She didn't look at me as she said it.

How, exactly, was I supposed to respond to *that*? It *had* affected my presentation, *and* it wrecked my dress, so obviously it wasn't "okay." But it seemed as if she was trying to apologize. Sort of.

"It turned out all right," I said, remembering that she'd had bigger problems the year before. "Thanks again for all the help and everything. And congratulations on the photography award."

She seemed to stand up straighter when she heard the compliment. "Thanks. I won a photo shoot. It probably would have been a better prize for someone like you who doesn't have very many pictures, but I got some contract offers, too, so now I'll be able to update my book for whomever I sign with. I've got four agencies that are interested." She smiled and waved a handful of business cards in front of me.

She was obviously right about the photos being of more

use to me, but I still couldn't figure out whether her comment was meant to be considerate or hurtful.

"That's really great," I said, closing up my suitcase. At that moment, my cell rang, and Shayla grabbed it from the nightstand beside her and handed it to me.

It was Gabriella, calling to tell me that she'd brought the car around to the front parking lot and that I should meet her there. I repeated her instructions back to her over the phone, then realized – too late – that Shayla was listening and looking out the window.

"I thought you said your dad's girlfriend was driving you home," she said evenly after I'd hung up.

"That's right."

"Well, I noticed when I passed you your phone that it said it was Gabriella calling. And I see her Jeep outside, where you were talking about meeting. So, is *she* your dad's girlfriend?"

There was no point in trying to hide it anymore. The convention was over – not that Gabriella had been one of the judges in my division anyway – and Shayla had already figured it out. Still, I tried to play it down. "Yeah. They've been going out a bit this summer. I don't know how serious it is."

"Wow. You're so lucky! I had to work super hard to get *my* contract offers. It sure would have helped to have had an inside track." She smiled. "Then again, at least I can feel good about doing it on my own. Hey, good luck with the agencies she – I mean – *you* got offers from."

"Good luck to you, too." I said, shaking a bit, but not knowing whether it was from anger or embarrassment.

"What's wrong?" Gabriella asked later as I loaded my stuff into her Jeep. My confusion over Shayla was apparently showing. "You should be as confident as the girl you were when you did the flawless runway routine yesterday!"

I knew she was right. "I am," I said. "It's just really hard to say goodbye to everyone." It wasn't a *lie* exactly; she just interpreted it differently than I meant.

I didn't call or message my parents on the way home because I wanted to wait to talk to them about everything in person.

What I didn't know at the time was that they both wanted to talk to me, too – about something more important than modeling.

# CHAPTER 21

When Gabriella and I arrived at my dad's, I saw that my mom's car was in the driveway. Dad greeted me with a hug and a kiss almost before I got the door open. Mom joined him, even though public displays of affection aren't usually her style, and the three of us had this weird "family hug" moment with Gabriella standing right behind us.

"So, how did it go?" my parents asked. I told them about the three offers I needed to consider. Even though both of them *said* all the right things – about being proud of me and knowing I could do it – I felt as if they were holding something back. It reminded me of the way Brandon had acted the night he said we needed "to talk."

I knew Mom would have been anxious to hear all about the convention, but I thought it was odd for her to be over at my dad's yet again. Normally, the dog hair alone would be enough to keep her away; adding in the regular presence of Dad's new girlfriend made it start to feel like a really bad reality show.

"Well, it certainly seems that we have a lot to think about and consider," Dad said, after we'd finished talking about the convention. Then he turned to my mom, but spoke to me. "Honey, your mother has some news of her own."

I wondered later whether Gabriella had been prepped for the news, or whether she just had good instincts, because she took that moment to make a quick exit, telling my dad she'd call him that night.

For an instant before she spoke, my mom's eyes flashed scared, but she regained control just as quickly. "Ashley, when you called on Friday afternoon and I wasn't at the office, it was because I'd just come from a doctor's appointment. I'm going to be starting chemotherapy in September," she explained.

"Chemotherapy?" My mouth went completely dry and I felt as if I needed to sit down, even though I was already sitting. I'd been totally prepared for a family conference about modeling or something, but it caught me off-guard to be talking about my mom's breast cancer. Guiltily, I realized that lately I'd been assuming everything always had to be about me. I put my hand over my eyes and focused on breathing. "I thought the surgery and radiation you already had were supposed to take care of everything."

"They were, darling, but they didn't quite do the job the doctors had hoped, so I'm going to have a little bit of chemotherapy. And then another round of radiation. And hopefully, that will take care of it, once and for all." Her voice was fake-hopeful, and I didn't trust it.

"Your mother and I have been talking about the arrangements for fall and whether we should stick to the regular schedule, or if you should perhaps come to my place full-time," my dad explained.

"I don't want you to feel like you're stuck taking care of me at my place if I'm sick," my mom said.

Everything about my world shifted in that single instant. I'd been terrified when I'd found out about her cancer in the first place, but my mom and the doctors had assured me that they "caught it early" and everything would be fine. My mom had spent months looking and acting fine, and even now, you couldn't tell by looking at her that there was anything wrong at all. So as much as I knew that things aren't always as they appear on the surface, I hadn't let myself believe that my mother could really be so sick that we were talking about chemotherapy, custodial changes, and – indirectly – everything bad that could happen after that.

I was totally used to leaving my mom to go to my dad's place – I even suspected that she kind of enjoyed having the privacy every couple of days. And I *knew* she liked to be independent, and that she wouldn't want me – or anyone else – fussing over her, but I also couldn't imagine her being home by herself when she was so sick.

"I can't exactly leave you home alone if you're not doing well," I said, taking my cue from them and staying calm on the outside, despite my panic underneath.

"I know that, Ashley," my mom said. "And it's possible that I won't actually get very ill from the treatments, so we're not deciding anything right now. Your father and I just wanted to alert you to the fact that there could be some changes happening in a few weeks or months."

My mom described the possible "changes" as if she was talking about light bulbs, not her life. I understood by her tone that the discussion was over and she didn't want to talk about it anymore. Her calm demeanor frustrated me a million times more than Brandon had with his excuses for why we shouldn't go out anymore.

I struggled to reconcile two very different pictures in my head. Everything I knew about my mom made me believe she'd be okay: she was physically strong, she was a positive thinker, she was a determined fighter. But I also knew that chemo could be brutal and that they didn't give it to you unless they were sure you needed it. And if you needed it, your cancer was still there.

All of a sudden her growing support of modeling made sense: she needed it for a distraction as much as I did. And, as Justin had predicted, I knew what I had to do.

* * *

After we'd talked things out as much as Mom would allow, I told my dad I wanted to go back to my mom's with her. He agreed, even though technically I was supposed to be with him. My mom tried to argue, telling me she was "fine," but I still didn't want her to be on her own. At least if it had been the other way around, my dad would have had Daphne, but without me, Mom would be totally alone.

Later that night, when my mom had gone to bed, I called Caitlyn and talked to her for a long time about my mom. The convention and Justin suddenly didn't seem as important anymore, but she wanted to hear about both of those things, too, so she suggested that I come over to her house the next day, when I'd finished at the shelter.

It was a relief to get back to the shelter to distract myself from my mom's health issues, and to make myself useful again. I still needed to be careful about scratches and bruises, so I mostly just cleaned litter boxes and dog pens, rather than spend a lot of time directly with the animals. I missed them. They were right there, but all I could say was "hello" and pet their heads gently. It wasn't the same as running around out in the yard with the dogs, or letting the kittens climb all over me.

I helped out in the office a bit, too, preparing last-minute mailings advertising the upcoming summer fundraiser – "The Doggy Paddle" – a short canoe race they hold every year. Participants collect pledges, or pay an entry fee, and then canoe down the river. Local businesses donate prizes and snacks at the finish line. Brandon and I had entered together the two previous years because of his love for canoeing, and that had been part of what had gotten me interested in volunteering at the shelter. When I'd learned that Brandon would be gone all summer – before we broke up – my mom had promised to do the race with me. That day at the shelter, I realized she wouldn't be physically up to canoeing. Before I knew it, I was crying all over the pile of envelopes I'd promised to stuff. And – for once – I wasn't even trying to stop myself.

I wasn't sobbing hard, the way I had done alone in my bed after Brandon and I had broken up. Hot tears were just sliding down my face, splatting onto the table in front of me. I was too scared for my mom, and too tired of pretending I wasn't, to even feel my usual deep level of public embarrassment when Natalie, the shelter manager, found me that way.

She came through the door to the office, saw me, and opened her mouth as if she was about to say something. Then she quickly closed the door behind her and left again. At first, I thought maybe I'd freaked her out, but when she came back in, wordlessly, and gently placed a little black purring machine onto my lap, I knew that she understood better than I did what I needed.

"She could use some comforting," Natalie said, and I wasn't sure whether she was talking to me about the cat, or to the cat about me.

I noticed that Raven had recently been spayed. Her little belly had been shaved, but her stitches were healing and she was as loving and cuddly as ever. I held her for a long time, until my tears had stopped, and then I headed over to Caitlyn's for some human interaction.

When I got there, Caitlyn and her baby sister, Angelique, were covered in chocolate pudding.

"I'm glad you made it," Caitlyn said, giving me little hug as I came in. "Want to paint with us?" she asked, motioning with her chin toward the kitchen counter, which was covered with pudding-smeared paper.

"Seriously? You're painting with pudding?"

Caitlyn nodded. "Finger-painting! When was the last

time you did *that*? It's really liberating," she said. "*And* totally non-toxic this way," she added as the baby stuffed all of her pudding-covered fingers into her mouth at once.

"So what do you do if you want to keep one of these masterpieces?" I asked, grabbing a sheet of slippery paper and dipping one finger cautiously into the pudding cup.

Angelique, propped up in her high chair, laughed as she painted Caitlyn's face. Already, I was glad I'd come, knowing the two of them would be just as good for me as Raven had been.

"We'll take digital photos of everything," Caitlyn explained as if it was the most obvious thing in the world. Last year she was all caught up in trying to make art that looked "real," which she is very good at, but lately she's been experimenting a lot more with different styles and subjects. She's so talented that even her pudding pictures – all brown and streaky – were fascinating. I should have known she'd already worked out a way to preserve everything.

I hadn't started with a plan for my pudding picture, but I found myself making hesitant horizontal squiggles across the page. Caitlyn was splattering pudding across her page with both hands simultaneously while Angelique giggled and squirmed delightedly and smacked her own pudding-covered hands against the page.

"I wouldn't have thought she'd be ready for art so young," I said, adding a shark fin to my picture. "But she seems to love it. You're an awesome sister."

"Thanks," she smiled. "It's messy now, but I want her to grow up confident."

"That's how she should be," I agreed, starting to feel tears in the corners of my eyes but still not coming up with the words to talk anymore about my fears for my mom. "Confident is definitely good." I'd added a stick figure to my painting and it looked like she was about to be lunch for the shark. Caitlyn glanced over at my page and smiled at me.

"Cautious is good, too," she said, and I knew she was summing up not just my painting, but almost everything I'd ever done. "Confidence puts you in with the sharks, but cautious means you have a boat somewhere, to get you away, even if you have to captain it yourself."

My boat wasn't much – just a flat little raft I'd popped up onto the waves because I felt sorry for my little stick figure – but Caitlyn saw its value.

"So … are you okay?" she asked, and I felt relieved to be with a friend who cared enough to ask but wouldn't push.

I nodded and stuck some chocolate-brown clouds up in the sky above the shark. "I guess. My mom and dad say the chemo's going to fix everything. They want me to be happy about the modeling, and not to worry," I explained.

"How *is* your mom?" she asked.

"Crazy. Driven. Totally reluctant to slow down, even though she's about to start chemo," I told her, then giggled. "The same as always, I guess."

"The same as *you*, you mean."

"Yeah." I knew she meant the "driven" part, but all day I felt as if I'd been leaning way more toward crazy.

"I don't think she's going to be able to do *The Doggy*

*Paddle* with me, though, like we'd planned. It's just a little race, but still … it sucks," I confessed.

I could tell by the look of concern on her face that she understood it wasn't just about me not having a partner, but she tried to help anyway. "Conner and I were talking about getting a canoe and entering together," she said. "But if you want, I could team up with you, even though I know it won't be the same as having your mom there."

Surprisingly, the offer cheered me up. Conner and Caitlyn had been friends for a long time and they were teaching arts and crafts together, part-time at a day camp. Doing one charity event as a team didn't mean for sure that they were becoming more than friends, but I was happy for her, in case it did. And I wasn't going to get in the way of it.

"No. You should go with Conner," I said. "I just thought of someone else who could do it." She blushed, and I had a feeling I was right about Conner – but that she wasn't going to give me a chance to ask her about it.

"Tell me all about the convention now," she insisted. "Starting with the guy you're going canoeing with."

So while we painted, I told her about Justin and Shayla and the excitement – which I hadn't really been able to enjoy – of being offered a modeling contract.

By the time we'd finished with the pudding, I was painting little black cats, instead of sharks.

"You know," I confessed, "this is kind of therapeutic."

"It really is," she said as she licked her fingers.

# CHAPTER 22

I called Justin later that night to invite him to The Doggy Paddle, and he sounded enthusiastic when I asked him to join me. I was pretty sure there were rules about who's supposed to phone who first, or how many times you were supposed to email and text message before calling a guy, but I figured that if any of that bothered him, he was going to be too high-maintenance for me.

"I've never been canoeing in my life," he said when I asked him, and I was afraid it meant he didn't want to try. "But it sounds really fun."

We made plans for him to drive down and meet me at my dad's place two weeks from Saturday, and I felt a little rush of excitement in anticipation of having another actual date. I'd forgotten that it had been like that with Brandon in the beginning, when seeing one another meant making plans ahead of time. After Brandon and I got completely comfortable with each other, we just *assumed* we'd get together, and then we figured out our plans at the last minute. I hadn't realized it at the time, but I'd missed the fun of thinking about the possibilities as I looked forward to going out.

Justin had decided to sign a contract with one of the agencies that had scouted him, and within a couple of days of the modeling convention and my mom's big announcement, I signed with an agency called *Vrais Visages*. It wasn't the largest, or the best known of the places that had been interested, but it was the closest – the most likely to get me good jobs without a lot of travel for now, and Gabriella said they were highly regarded within the industry. While modeling schools like hers could book models for the occasional newspaper flyer or mall fashion show, *Vrais Visages* worked with clients who had larger budgets and more specific needs.

Despite Gabriella's insistence that it was a promising agency, and *my* explanation that I liked the idea of getting more personalized attention in a smaller place, my mother suspected that her being sick had played a part in my decision. She pressured me to reconsider.

"You have to do what's best for *you*," she said, though all things considered, I personally thought I had. "I don't want my cancer to affect your future," she said. *That* had to be one of the dumbest things I'd ever heard. I mean, seriously – whether she got better or worse, just knowing my mom had faced something like that was *obviously* going to affect me for the rest of my life.

I tried to reassure her. "I'm happy with my choice, and I think I'm well on the way to achieving the challenge I'd set for myself at the beginning of the summer. Plus, this way, the travelling won't be as disruptive when I'm back in school," I said. But the tense set of her jaw every time I mentioned *Vrais Visages* told me she wasn't convinced.

"She'll come around," my father said later. And, it turned out, it happened sooner than I'd expected. Gabriella had arranged for the local paper to do an interview with me, and it totally changed my mom's mind and lifted her mood.

Within a few days of me signing, a reporter named Danielle came to my mom's house to meet with me. She'd already researched *Vrais Visages* and was able to quote some of the ad campaigns they'd provided models for.

"They're a really excellent agency," Danielle gushed, echoing what I already knew from Gabriella and from my own research. "So – how is it that *you* were able to catch their attention?" She sat back and waited for me to answer. As I talked about the convention, she eyed me up and down, seemingly searching for that "special something" that everyone seemed to think I had. I was tempted to admit that I didn't exactly see it, either, but instead I tried to emphasize the hard work I'd put into practicing my walk, and how I'd had to really cut back on my shelter involvement. She asked me some interesting questions then about shelter animals being judged on their appearances and whether or not it bothered me to be getting involved with an industry that treated people the same way. *That* question led to a long discussion about "black dog syndrome," and how the dark animals always end up being the last ones to get adopted. She was easy to talk to, and I got the feeling that she was being careful to understand who I really was.

When the article appeared, though, the headline was "Model Perfect." *Ugh!* It was humiliating. I was completely embarrassed to have a headline like that over my picture, and I could just imagine how it was going to look to everyone at school.

At that point, my mom – who had been doubtful about my choice of agency and had initially been worried about me getting sidetracked by modeling – also began humiliating me in that special way that only a mother can. First, she called all the neighbors, *supposedly* to have them save extra copies of the story – even though I told her she could have just downloaded it off the newspaper's website. *Then,* she mailed the cut-out newspaper copies off to all my aunts and uncles, even though I'd told her *again* that she could have just emailed them the link.

I know moms are supposed to be proud of their kids, but it seemed kind of *braggish* to me, and I didn't know which was worse – Overly Concerned Mom or Overly Enthusiastic Mom.

Overenthusiastic Gabriella was also starting to become an issue. "This is excellent exposure, Ashley," Gabriella said the night the article came out. I wondered whether she meant it was excellent for *me*, or for *her*, because I already had a contract. The part about how I'd gotten started was probably good advertising for her modeling school.

She was over at my dad's *again*, and even though she wasn't coaching me anymore, she still tended to dominate the conversations. It was getting hard to remember a time when

*I'd* been the one with the significant other who was always over and my *dad* was the one who was the third wheel.

"They used your best portfolio shot, and they really did a wonderful job explaining how you fit into all the current trends in modeling," she babbled on and on.

I *was* relieved that the article had won my mom over and that Gabriella felt it was so well done. The story didn't talk about anything *except* my "budding" modeling career, though, and it reminded me of Shayla's comment about how it would be weird to read a novel with you on the cover if the book wasn't about you. Danielle didn't end up writing about any of the stuff I'd told her about the shelter. Or, if she *had* included it, the editor had taken it out. The girl she described in the article sounded a lot more like Shayla than me.

Deep down, I knew that the real problem with everyone gushing about my new modeling "success" was that I hadn't actually had any success yet. It made me feel like a fraud. Even though my mom and dad and Gabriella – and even the newspaper – were making a big deal about me signing with *Vrais Visages*, it didn't really count for anything as far as I was concerned if I wasn't getting any modeling work.

Not that I hadn't been trying. Within days of signing my contract – which basically said they'd attempt to get jobs for me, then take twenty-five percent of whatever I earned – they'd started sending me on go-sees.

The first go-see was for a high-end department store flyer. They needed teens to model their fall lines. The agency told me it was low-paying but that most girls started with that kind of work.

Apparently, nobody had mentioned that fact to the guy who was booking the models. "We need more experienced girls," he said when he saw that my portfolio only had a few shots in it. "It's an all-day shoot, with a lot of costume changes, and we don't have the time to talk you through. *Plus,* your hair is a little too 'edgy' for us – we want more *wholesome,* more girl-next-door."

The next go-see, for a jewellery company, wasn't any better. "We were looking for someone more – willowy," they said. "Someone who would be more believable as a fortune teller." *I can be a fortune teller!* I wanted to scream. *I predict great things for your company if you hire me!* I could see it, but somehow, they couldn't.

It went on like that a couple of times a day for a couple of weeks. As certain as *Vrais Visages* had been about me at the convention when they'd offered to represent me, I didn't seem to be fitting in with any of their clients' ideas of what they wanted in a model.

"Too mature," said the teen magazine editor.

"Too young looking," said the lingerie store owner.

"Too athletic," said the fashion designer.

"Are you sure you're doing everything Gabriella recommended?" my father asked on one of the rare occasions when she wasn't around. *Yes, Dad,* I thought. *I don't have any weird tan lines – I don't have a tan at all because I never go outside. I hardly ever get to feel kitten fur on my hands anymore because I don't have any time to go to the shelter, and I'm not supposed to get*

*scratched anyway. I go to bed WAY too early for a teenager in the*
*summer, because I can't have bags under my eyes, and I have to get*
*up so early every morning to get into the city and sit around all day*
*waiting to hear from the casting people about everything that's*
*wrong with me...* I *thought* all this, but I didn't want to seem
ungrateful, so what I *said* was "I don't know. I'll ask her the
next time I see her. These aren't Gabriella's clients anymore,
though, so maybe they want something different than what
she had seen."

Mom left Gabriella out of it entirely and directed all of
her concerns at *me*.

"You're not going out covered in dog hair like that, are
you?" she asked as I arrived back at her place from my dad's
one night. I wasn't, and it really bugged me that she'd ask me
that, because I am *so* careful about it when I am out in public.
Plus, I wasn't exactly *covered* in it. It was really just one strand
that I could have picked up anywhere.

"Or maybe you're not projecting enough enthusiasm,"
she suggested later, as I told her about another rejection. "You
know that what you put out there into the universe is the same
thing that comes back around to you later."

All of the "universe" talk left me wondering more and
more why my mom had gotten sick. I knew it was normal to
question why you got cancer and to try to figure out ways to
get better. Still, she'd read a lot of books when she was
diagnosed about healing through "the power of positive
thinking," but she hadn't gotten better, and now she needed
chemo. Did it mean that she wasn't trying hard enough (and

that I wasn't either, at my go-sees?), or did it just mean that sometimes, no matter how much the two of us tried to control things, some things were actually out of our hands?

Of course, I *didn't* say any of that stuff out loud. I knew that if positive vibes really *were* the answer, she'd see me as a failure for questioning their value and not being as certain as she was that you could change your circumstances by thinking positively.

The thing was, I'd been *positive* that Brandon and I were meant to be together and it hadn't worked out that way. But now, I often found myself checking for messages from Justin and thinking about *him* a lot. I'd been counting down the days until the Doggy-Paddle.

I'd picked out what I was going to wear days in advance, even though it was just shorts and the shelter T-shirt I'd won during the same race the year before. I put my hair up in a messy bun that I hoped looked casual but also kind of mature. It was a lot like the go-sees I'd been doing, because I didn't want it to seem as if I was trying too hard, but I also didn't want it to seem as if I didn't care, either.

Still, when Justin arrived at my dad's for the race, I found myself melting all over again at the sight of him, and wishing I *had* been able to dress up a little more – even though we were only going paddling. He was also dressed in shorts and a T-shirt, but his agents obviously hadn't warned *him* about getting a tan – he was bronze all over. I could also tell from his bare legs and arms that he'd been working out. Seeing again how gorgeous he was, I forgot for a second that we actually had lots of things in common, and I caught myself wondering if maybe I'd just been seduced by his looks.

Two seconds after he'd come in, though, I remembered what it was that I'd liked so much about his personality. He flashed me a huge, playful grin and picked me right up off the floor as he hugged me. As soon as he'd put me back down, he bent over to meet Daphne.

"Ashley didn't tell me you were so beautiful!" he said to her in a mock whisper. "I have a Lollie-pup at home who is going to be *very* jealous when he finds out how pretty you are!"

Daphne wagged her tail so hard that her entire back end swung from side to side while he rubbed her head and ears.

Dad came in just then with an expression of mock horror. "Ashley, we've talked about this! You can't just keep bringing home strays!"

Justin was back up on his feet and shaking my dad's hand in no time. "Don't worry, sir," he said, having totally picked up on my dad's weird sense of humor. "I don't bark, I'm perfectly housebroken, and I've been completely de-wormed."

"Well, then you're not Ashley's type *at all*," my dad teased back. "But her mother is going to love you."

She *was* going to love him. I could tell my dad did already. How could anyone not admire the way Justin was able to act totally crazy while meeting the parents, but still seem completely real?

We spent a couple of minutes at my dad's house, then headed out to meet my mom because she'd insisted on taking

Justin and me out for lunch before the race. Obviously, it was an excuse for her to meet the new guy, even though she tried to pretend it was a "thank you" for him taking her place in the canoe. Dad and I were very familiar with her tactics and secretly called it "motherly-meddling masquerading as a meal."

As Dad had sarcastically predicted, it didn't take long for Justin to win Mom over, too. I'm not sure if it was because of the things I'd already told him, or because he was good at reading people, but he seemed to know that my mom valued different things than my dad. He listened to her respectfully, talked about his hope to be a lawyer, and shared some interesting factoids about modeling.

"He's wonderful, Ashley," she whispered as she hugged me good-bye.

Such high praise from someone who'd always insisted that I have high standards of my own helped me believe a little bit more in what she'd said about "putting good things out into the universe" so they could come back to you.

* * *

Caitlyn and Conner had gotten a couple of canoes for us to use, and they were waiting for us at the designated Doggy Paddle starting line when we arrived. As I made the introductions, I noticed that – ever the *artistes*! – they both had dressed for the occasion in matching dog collars. Conner's was double-looped into a bracelet, and Caitlyn had wrapped hers around her hair like a headband. They'd used puffy fabric paint to add little paw prints and bone shapes to plain collars. "We thought it would be fun to get into the spirit of the event," Caitlyn explained, "so Conner came over last night to help me make them. We're planning to leave them with the shelter for some of their dogs when we're done."

"You know, you guys could probably sell a bunch of those and make a lot of money," Justin told them. "People are always happy to pay for original works of art, and you could donate a portion of the proceeds to the shelter."

Conner was interested in Justin's idea, and the guys started talking about organizing a custom collar business while Caitlyn and I gave each other thumbs up approval for potential boyfriend compatibility.

"Okay, guys," I said to Conner and Caitlyn later as we floated toward the starting line in our canoes. "I want to win again this year, so don't be surprised if our canoe goes whizzing by and you don't see us again until the end of the race."

"Why are we trying so hard to win?" Justin interrupted.

"Because it's a race," I said.

"So?"

"So we have to go fast!"

"But if we go fast, we won't be able to talk to each other, and we'll miss all the little froggies and everything else along the way." He pretended to sulk.

"He's totally right," Conner said with a little half-smile. "Froggies are cool."

"What do we win if we get there first?" Justin asked.

"Nothing big – just T-shirts like this one," I motioned to

the one I was wearing. "Maybe a mug or a water bottle. Whatever the sponsors have donated."

"So, what if I promise to buy you a T-shirt later, if we can take our time instead?" Justin offered. "You know, so we'll be able to enjoy the ride."

Obviously, I didn't need a T-shirt, or a water bottle. I was just used to paddling as fast as I could because Brandon and I were both competitive people who liked to win. Until Justin suggested it, it hadn't actually occurred to me that it would be okay – enjoyable, even – to just go slowly and enjoy each other's company at the same time.

In the end, the four of us did decide to go slow, and the race that Brandon and I had won in forty-two minutes the year before stretched on through most of the afternoon. We paddled leisurely enough for turtles to look on calmly as we drifted by, and for dragonflies to rest on the sides of our canoes. Justin and I tried unsuccessfully to tip Caitlyn and Conner out of their boat, but they managed to dunk the two of us. I emerged from the water laughing, not caring about the possibility of sunburn or bruises, and feeling truly happy for the first time since all the prep work for the modeling convention started. It wasn't normally like me to relax, but that day, it felt good to be someone else.

* * *

Two and a half weeks later, I got another letter from Brandon.

*August 20th*

*Dear Ashley,*

*My mom told me about seeing you at the mall, and she also sent me the article. I couldn't believe it. (Not because you aren't pretty enough, but just because I never knew modeling was something you wanted to do, and it still feels weird that we have been out of touch so much that I don't know what's going on in your life). I don't really know how to write this, but I guess you probably figured out by now that my mom didn't make me break up with you. I just couldn't stand seeing you so upset after I said we should take a break, so I thought maybe it would help if you thought it wasn't all my fault. I would still like to talk to you when I get home. As you know, I'll be back on the 29th.*

*Your friend, Brandon*

*P.S. Tell Daphne I said "hi" and give her an ear-scratch for me.*

I noticed that not only had he apologized for the lie about his mother – and explained it, which helped, too – but he'd also switched from "Sincerely" to "Your friend." Most incredibly, though, I found that I could read his letter and just feel only a bit sad about us, instead of completely crushed. If I'd had more time before his return home, I would have written him back. By the time I received the letter, his return was only a few days away.

I thought about what I would say when I saw him again, and I told Daphne "hi" as he'd asked me to do. Just as I was about to scratch her ears, my cell rang. It was *Vrais Visages*, calling to tell me I'd finally booked a job.

*Pava* was a high-end fashion retailer I'd done a go-see for during the prior week. Their clothes weren't exactly affordable, but they were gorgeous. Even though it was only August, they were ready to shoot their Christmas ads, and they wanted me to be one of their *Pava girls*.

I was cool and professional on the phone while I got the details, but after I'd hung up, I grabbed Daphne by the front paws and danced her around the room. Then, I called or texted almost everyone I cared about.

"That's amazing, honey," my dad said when I told him about it later that afternoon. "I knew you could do it," my mom said, as if she'd never doubted me. "Go be awesome," Caitlyn told me. "U roc," Justin texted. And, finally, Gabriella shrieked, "This will be huge!"

Though I went to bed early the night before because I wanted to look refreshed, it was hard to sleep. I spent most of the night obsessing about new poses I could try and whether or not I'd be able to keep it fluid.

Two days after I'd received the call, *Pava* sent a car to pick me up to take me into the city. I'd swallowed my pride again and asked Gabriella directly for advice, which I rehearsed in my head all the way to the studio.

I was feeling confident and totally ready when I arrived – until I entered the studio and saw the other girl they'd cast.

# CHAPTER 23

The look of horror on Shayla's face when she saw me told me instantly that she hadn't expected me, either, and that there was no way the butt glue had been an accident.

"Hi, Shayla," I said, wanting to be professional despite the sick feeling in my stomach.

"Hello Ash-*lee*," she trilled as if my name was a bird call, before hissing like an angry snake under her breath. "Did they send a car for you, too, or did you get a ride with your dad's girlf – I mean, Gabriella – again?"

"I came in the car, thanks for asking," I said, pretending to be oblivious to her insinuation. "Justin will be so excited to hear that you got a contract, too."

She sniffed and flicked her hair over her shoulder before turning back to face the lighted mirror. She stared at her reflection and spoke calmly. "Just wait until you see the wardrobe they've picked out for us – *it's to die for*."

We didn't talk anymore throughout the hair and make-up session, though her eyes seemed to narrow whenever she looked my way. I told myself I was lucky to have landed the same photography job as Shayla so early in my modeling career, and that her jealousy was actually a compliment to me. I also thought about how much it was going to mean to my mother to see me achieve some real success.

I was *Invincible Ashley*.

Until I saw the wardrobe.

The "wardrobe" – their holiday line – was a soft black sweater for me, and a rich deep red one for Shayla. Each sweater was shaped to fit at the waist. And appallingly, each sweater was trimmed at the neck and cuffs with black fur. My stomach churned and heaved, and my head felt both light and heavy at the same time.

"This is *so* soft!" Shayla exclaimed, rubbing the sweater cuff against her forearm. "I bet it's as soft as those animals you work with at the shelter, isn't it Ashley?"

Her expression held a challenge. I could tell she was waiting to see if I would take the bait.

Ignoring her, I turned to the stylist, a woman with dark red hair cut very short against her head.

"Is this the only wardrobe?" I knew it was a dumb question – obviously they'd thought carefully about every aspect of their ad campaign. They knew what products they wanted to sell, and those were the outfits we'd be wearing. Still, I was trying to buy myself some time to think.

"No – we've got some outerwear, and a couple of vests … we're doing quite a few of our luxury lines today," she said. I glanced over to the rack she'd indicated and saw that all of the coats and vests were also fur-trimmed!

Shayla was still looking at me with raised eyebrows, and

she spoke to me the way she had when I'd first met her – as if we were friends. "Come on, Ash, let's try these on." She picked up the sweater I was supposed to wear and held it out to me.

I took it back behind the screen where we were meant to change, and I tried to be professional about the whole thing – *especially* with Shayla there. I undid my blouse, told myself that it was just a job and that sometimes there are things involved in jobs that you don't like or don't agree with. I knew some jobs could be unpleasant, but I always did what was expected of me. Most importantly, I told myself that it was probably fake fur.

As I pulled the sweater on over my head, though, I realized that it smelled ever so faintly like Daphne, after she's been shampooed.

The sick feeling in my stomach that I'd been trying to suppress now filled me completely, and I knew I couldn't hold it back any longer. I flung the sweater back over my head, tossed it on a chair behind me, and ran out into the studio, gagging. Barely to the sink, I heaved and threw up, knowing my hair and make-up – and possibly, my reputation – would be ruined if I couldn't get it together and put the sweater on.

"Are you okay?" the stylist asked, looking a little sick herself. I held onto the sink and teetered above it with my head down, not caring that I was in my bra, and absolutely hating the idea of wearing dead animals.

Out of the corner of my eye, I saw Shayla emerge from behind the screen wearing *her* sweater and looking smug.

"Most girls do their puking *before* they show up to work," she said. "It's a good thing you didn't ruin the sweater."

"I just … I didn't know we'd be wearing fur," I started to explain as I ran some water into the sink to clean it out.

"It's beautiful, isn't it?" Shayla said, stroking her sweater. "But the label doesn't say what kind it is. You're the animal expert, Ashley, what do *you* think?" She looked at me innocently, and I realized that that was part of what made her such a good model – she could play any role she wanted.

"I - I don't know – m-maybe rabbit," I stuttered, my throat burning with stomach acid.

"Or mink? Or chinchilla?" she was still stroking one of her cuffs as if it was a pet, while I stood there feeling like a trapped animal. Then suddenly I saw another familiar face.

"Mom! What are you doing here?" Trust her to choose this one time to skip work and check up on me. "I was just on my way from a doctor's appointment and I thought I'd come by and see your first professional shoot," she explained. "If that's okay?" She looked around at the others: Shayla, dressed and ready to go, the stylist and the photographer whispering and likely trying to figure out what to do about my barfing episode, and me, in my bra, with my hair messed up and what must have been a look of total confusion.

"Yeah, sure," I managed to mutter as I passed her. "I – I'm just not feeling very well. I was just sick in the sink. I have to get dressed." I made my way back in behind the screen.

"What? But you're okay, right." I guess the word "right" was supposed to make it interrogative, but there wasn't really any question in her voice. She could do cancer and still go to work – *surely* her daughter could throw up and then pose for a few pictures.

The stylist sounded more annoyed than concerned. "So, are you going to be okay?" she asked. "Because if we need to get another girl in, I need to let the agency know *now*."

I carefully picked up the sweater from where I'd tossed it on the chair, and I looked at the label. *Genuine fur trim*, it said. It didn't say what kind, but the idea of it grossed me out.

I couldn't remember ever letting someone down. I didn't have perfect attendance at school like my mother had had, but I did take my commitments seriously.

"I'm sorry, but I won't wear this," I said, coming out and handing the sweater back to the stylist.

My mother looked around. "I don't understand."

The stylist threw her arms up. "Me either! It's a beautiful piece – why are you holding everyone up?" She frowned, and when I didn't answer, she put her hands back on her hips and turned to my mother as if to say "She's *your* daughter – *you* talk some sense into her."

By this time, Mom had clued in that it was the fur freaking me out. She crossed the room and picked up the sweater. Holding it toward me, she spoke quietly. "Ashley, this is a beautiful, high-end piece of clothing, and it will look gorgeous on you."

"Mom, you know I want to make you proud, but I won't wear fur." I was starting to shake again, and they could all hear it in my voice.

"Oh, please!" Shayla approached us and interjected. "You just started modeling, you've been offered a major ad campaign, and you're worried about the product they want you to sell? What's your deal?"

I shrugged, knowing it was likely that *nobody* would understand, no matter how I tried to explain it. "It just seems kind of ... arrogant ... to wear fur."

"And you're not being arrogant standing here telling everyone else why you have a problem with a sweater," Shayla was practically screaming, "when a hundred other girls wanted this job?"

"You *did* sign a contract, Ashley," my mother reminded me.

I turned again to the stylist, shaky, but sure. "You need to call in one of those other girls."

"I can't believe this! You know you'll be blacklisted, right?" she said, pulling out a cell phone and jabbing at it with her fingernails.

"Wait here!" my mother spoke sharply to me and followed the stylist across the room.

Shayla smirked, then spoke in a baby voice, mocking me. "Poor Ashley! She's so good and she doesn't drink and she loves all the little animals, but she always does exactly what her mommy tells her to do, so now she's going to have to wear the furry sweater even though she doesn't want to ..."

"No," I said. "I *won't* have to wear it, because I don't need this job. Feeling good about myself and my decision is worth way more than *looking good* to everyone else."

I re-buttoned my blouse with quaking fingers, knowing I'd have to stand up to my mother again *and* explain all to my dad and Gabriella. I was also certain that *Vrais Visages* would drop me.

Shayla looked at me the way I'd been looking at the dead things they'd asked me to model, but I thought I heard something soft, and maybe apologetic, behind her words. "This campaign can still make your career," she said as I walked out past her. "Open your eyes."

"I just did," said "Awesome Ashley."

* * *

"I need some water or something," I said on the way out of the studio, with my throat still burning. Mom dug through her purse and came up with a mint as she followed me down the stairs. "You're one hundred percent sure about not doing this?" my mother asked in a tight voice. "Totally sure? One hundred percent?"

"No," I admitted when we got outside. "I'm *ninety-five percent* sure, and the other five percent doesn't want to disappoint you." My hands were still trembling and my voice cracked a little bit more when I said the last part.

She gave me an exasperated "why-don't-you-know-how-much-I-love-you" look and drew me into a hug. "Darling, I'd be disappointed if you did something you'd end up regretting," she whispered. "But never ever think that I would be disappointed in you for standing up for what you believe in."

"Even though they're probably going to blacklist me?" I asked. "Or sue me for breach of contract?"

"They won't sue you," she said with certainty. "And you'll be able to hold your head up high even if you don't ever model again."

Relief and exhaustion pushed out the fear and anxiety I'd been feeling. "I'm so glad you were there!" I sobbed into her shoulder.

"You're a strong, capable young woman, Ashley, and you would have been fine, whether I'd been there or not," she said, patting me on the back. "But I'm glad I was there, too, and I'm sorry I haven't been there for you more this summer."

I pulled back out of the hug and saw that she had tears in her eyes. "I didn't really want to ask you," I admitted.

"I know," she smiled as she hugged me again. "And I haven't exactly been very good about asking *you* for help, either," she acknowledged. "I'm going to try to be better at it, starting today."

My mom continued, still business-like, the way I knew and loved her, but also kind of cheerful in a way I hadn't seen for a long time. "There was actually another reason I came by this afternoon – I wanted to talk to you about something. Lately, I've been finding it really quiet when you're at your dad's." I braced myself, thinking she was about to tell me she'd found a new boyfriend. I didn't know how many crazy-in-love parents I could take, but then she surprised me.

"And being sick has really helped me see that maybe

having a spotless house isn't the most important thing in life," she continued. "Gabriella and I talked about that one night – how being sick changes your priorities."

I realized she wasn't talking about a boyfriend after all and I hoped I was right about what she was going to say next.

"So I was thinking about that little black cat at the shelter you'd mentioned. The one you were so worried about because of her color?"

"Raven!" I looked up at her, hoping my gut was right.

"Raven. Do you know if she's still up for adoption? Would she be a good choice for us, do you think?"

"She'd be perfect, Mom," I said.

I smiled, remembering how Brandon had promised me I'd find her a good home.

# CHAPTER 24

Mom was only allergic to dogs – not cats – but I'd never expected her to let one into our home. Suddenly, I sounded like the parent. "You're sure you can deal with a litter box when I'm at Dad's? And the cat fur on your clothes and scratches on the furniture?" I quizzed her. "You're not just doing this to make me happy?"

"No. I'm doing it because I think loosening up a bit and caring for a pet will make *me* happy."

"I think you're right," I said. Then, I called Natalie at the shelter and asked her to start the paperwork for Raven's adoption.

The excitement of picking up little Raven had taken the edge off of my memories of the sweater show-down, so I was almost surprised when my cell phone buzzed a couple of hours later as we pulled out of the shelter with our new little bundle of fur. Gabriella had sent me a text message.

What happened???

I could almost feel her shock through the phone. I typed back.

Come 2 my dads l8r. We need 2 talk.

"Do you want me to come in with you?" Mom asked as she dropped me off at Dad's place. "For support?"

I shook my head. "No, you need to get Raven home," I said. "I'm nervous, but *she's* freaking out." Like most of the cats I'd met at the shelter, she wasn't happy to be in a car. She didn't stop meowing the whole way.

Dad and Gabriella were waiting for me out on the deck when I arrived. I sat on a lounge chair and let Daphne climb up to sprawl across my lap as I explained everything.

By the time I'd finished, Gabriella had both hands locked tight across her forehead, as if she was trying to hold all of her angry thoughts inside. It didn't help.

"Did you really think about what you were doing?" she demanded. "What you were walking away from? We talked about this, Ashley – I know you love animals, but we can't let that interfere with your success."

Gabriella was pleading now, and I thought she might cry. I hadn't realized how personal it had become for her, but I remembered her telling me how impressed she'd been by my dad's continued support of my mom. I understood now that she was trying to be supportive of him, through me.

"Animals don't interfere with my life – they enrich it," I said. "Like you've done! I've spent my whole life trying to be what everyone else expected me to be, and I don't think I would have had the guts to walk away today if you hadn't told me about pursuing your passions."

My dad tilted his head slightly toward her, and she seemed to relax, though he took over the arguments, trying to outwit me with logic. "You know you aren't really going to be able to impact the fur industry just by refusing to be in one ad? They'll hire someone else and continue to sell the product."

"I know they'll still sell them," I acknowledged. "Just like I know I can't personally save all of the animals at the shelter, but every time I advocate for adopting a rescue animal, I do make a difference."

My dad seemed to understand, but I think he still felt sorry for Gabriella, too. "Gabriella did so much for you – she put in extra time, teaching you how to walk down a runway, helping you sign with an agency. You made a commitment, Ashley – how can you just walk away from it?"

"The first commitment I made this summer was to help animals," I said, rubbing Daphne's belly. "And," I added, reciting an anonymous quote Brandon had emailed me once: "I've always wanted to be as good a person as my dog thinks I am."

# CHAPTER 25

"You *what*?" Justin sputtered when I filled him in on everything later that night. We'd already had plans for him to visit, because I thought I'd have an exciting tale of modeling glory – instead of modeling mutiny – to share.

I repeated my news and waited in the uncharacteristic silence that followed.

"Wow," he said. "I didn't see *that* one coming."

"Shayla, either," I laughed, and he laughed with me.

"So what happens now – with *Vrais Visages*, I mean?" he asked.

"I don't really know yet," I confessed. "The *Pava* job is gone, obviously, but the agency called late this afternoon, and it turns out they aren't quite as pissed off as I'd expected. The woman I talked to said they were actually thinking of developing some corporate guidelines so that their clients would have to disclose upfront whether or not they use fur. That way none of their other models will end up having to make the on-the-spot decision I did."

"So there's still a chance that you can stay with the agency *and* affect change? Not many people would have had the guts to do what you did, *or* the luck to have it turn out so well. I *told* you there was something special about you. I'm really proud of you."

"Thanks." It was nice to know other people respected my decision, but more and more, I was finding that it was even better to know I could respect myself for it.

"Which is why I feel very mixed about the news *I* have to share," he said slowly, taking my hand in his and looking me right in the eye. "My agency got me a six-month gig overseas. It's great money, which will help out with school later on, and it'll give me a chance to travel. I think I'm going to take a semester off and go."

This time, it was Justin who waited in the silence. Had I heard his news four weeks earlier, I would have wondered why all the guys I liked were taking off for months at a time. A *week* earlier, and I would have wondered what I was doing wrong, and why I didn't have that kind of modeling offer. But that night, I was able to feel proud of myself for being okay with letting him go.

"Good for you," I said. "You should totally do it." And even though I knew I would miss him, I completely meant it.

\* \* \*

As always, Caitlyn was sympathetic about everything when I told her about it all the next day.

"So, are you and Justin going to keep in touch while he's away?" she asked.

"We're going to keep in touch by text and email, for sure. But we weren't *really* going out seriously yet anyway, and I'm still not sure I want to be in an actual relationship again right now. So I told him I wanted to be really clear that we can both see other people!"

She laughed, at first, but then she was serious. "I think that when Brandon gets back tomorrow, he's going to see that *you're* a whole other person than the one he left."

I wondered if Brandon had changed, too, and I hoped he wasn't angry that I hadn't written back.

I knew we'd be okay when he texted me the next day and asked me to meet him back in the schoolyard, at the hill where we'd started our summer by ending our relationship.

I took Daphne with me, knowing that if things felt awkward, she could bridge them for us the way she had at the beginning of "us." She recognized Brandon immediately and started pulling me toward him.

"Hey," he said as we approached, obviously unsure of how I was going to react to seeing him. Not having answered either of his letters seemed petty of me now, but I reminded myself that I had done the best I could for myself at the time, and nobody can expect more than that. Even me.

"You look great," I said honestly as I gave him a little hug. He was tanned and all the canoeing had filled out the muscles in his upper body – but more than that, he looked happy. Happy to see me.

"You, too," he hesitated, but then he found some words. "I missed you. All this funny stuff happened at camp, and I wanted to write to you about it. And then my mom told me you were modeling, and I really wanted to ask you about that. Not being able to talk to you every day, or even write to you about it … it was just weird."

"I know," I said. "There was lots of stuff I wanted to share with you, too," I said.

"So tell me now," he said as he smiled the smile I knew so well and had loved so much. "Tell me the most important thing about your summer."

For a moment, I considered it all: my mom's cancer, the animal shelter, the modeling.

All of it, somehow, seemed to come back to one thing.

"My mom adopted a cat from the shelter," I told him. "Raven – the black one. Remember the one I told you about before?"

He listened quietly and rubbed Daphne's belly while I explained the best things about my mom's new cat.

"She's so soothing," I said. "She sits on my mom's lap, and then because Mom feels bad disturbing her, my 'never-stops-moving' mother now sits still. It's kind of like forced relaxation. It turns out she enjoys it. We both do, actually. Who knew?" I wished she hadn't had to get sick to slow down, but I was happy that she was taking the time to re-evaluate some things. If we were lucky, *that* would be the biggest impact her illness would have on both of our lives.

"So, have you given any thought to changing Raven's name? So that the inter-species thing doesn't make her confused about who she is?"

Obviously, it was a hypothetical question, but I considered it anyway. "If Raven could actually know and understand her name, I think she'd be totally cool with it," I said as I reached for Daphne. "People love dogs most when they're fun, loyal, and trainable. Cats often don't *appear* to have those qualities. But I just don't think they need anyone's praise to feel secure. And," I added, "sometimes it's the stuff you can't see that makes the biggest difference."

You've met Ashley ... now hear her best friend's story:
# Painting Caitlyn
The debut novel from **Kimberly Joy Peters**

**Selected, International Reading Association "Young Adults' Choices" Reading List**

**Selected, YALSA "Quick Pick for Reluctant Young Adult Readers"**

## Painting Caitlyn
**978-1-897073-40-7**

**Available now!**

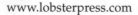

www.lobsterpress.com

## About the author:

Author and teacher **Kimberly Joy Peters** grew up in Southern Ontario. After winning top-ten honors in the *Toronto Star* Short Story Contest, she began to write professionally. She teaches French and art in Beaverton, Ontario, a town near the shores of Lake Simcoe. Visit Kimberly at www.kimberlyjoypeters.com.